Prai...
L...
BELIEVING

To remember what you've read, write your initials in a square!

AWAKENING

"The story is light and brief..." —817

DATE DUE		5/17
"Readers 6/9/17 mpatient for the next installment."		
Publishers Weekly		
"Characters are sharply drawn, and kids who like stories with psychic underpinnings will certainly appreciate the otherworldly goings-on and Callas reactions to them."		
B...W...		
"Deft characterization couples with a compelling plot in a somewhat unique setting to create appeal particularly to young teens seeking guidance and maturity in the face of life's difficulties." —*VOYA*		
"If you love suspense, you'll love this book."		
—Raven Blu, *VOYA* teen reviewer		

BOOKS BY WENDY CORSI STAUB

THE LILY DALE SERIES:

AWAKENING

BELIEVING

CONNECTING

DISCOVERING

LILY DALE
BELIEVING

WENDY CORSI STAUB

Walker & Company
New York

While Lily Dale, New York, is a real place, all the characters in this novel are fictional,
having been created solely by the author and not based on real people, living or dead.

First published in the United States of America in 2008 by
Walker Publishing Company, Inc.
Mass market edition published in 2009

Visit Walker & Company's Web site at www.walkeryoungreaders.com

For information about permission to reproduce selections from this book, write to
Permissions, Walker & Company, 175 Fifth Avenue, New York, New York 10010

The Library of Congress has cataloged the hardcover edition as follows:
Staub, Wendy Corsi.
Lily Dale : believing / Wendy Corsi Staub.
p.   cm.
Summary: After realizing that she shares her grandmother's psychic abilities, Calla
decides to stay with her in Lily Dale, the spiritualist community where her mother grew
up, even though her visions seem to be leading her toward danger.
ISBN-13: 978-0-8027-9656-1 • ISBN-10: 0-8027-9656-7 (hardcover)
[1. Psychic abilities—Fiction. 2. Psychics—Fiction. 3. Grandmothers—Fiction.
4. Lily Dale (N.Y.)—Fiction. 5. Mystery and detective stories.]
I. Title. II. Title: Believing.
PZ7.S804Lil 2007   [Fic]—dc22   2007032182

ISBN-13: 978-0-8027-9657-8 • ISBN-10: 0-8027-9657-5 (mass market)

Typeset by Westchester Book Composition
Printed in the U.S.A. by Worldcolor Buffalo
2 4 6 8 10 9 7 5 3

All papers used by Walker & Company are natural, recyclable products made from
wood grown in well-managed forests. The manufacturing processes conform to the
environmental regulations of the country of origin.

Dedicated to my newest little nephew, Harry,
aka Harrison Paul Sypko

And to Brody, Morgan, and Mark

The author is grateful to agents Laura Blake Peterson and Holly Frederick, as well as to Tracy Marchini, all at Curtis Brown, Ltd.; to Nancy Berland, Elizabeth Middaugh, and staff at Nancy Berland Public Relations; to Rick and Patty Donovan and Phil Pelleter at the Book Nook in Dunkirk, New York; to Emily Easton, Deb Shapiro, and everyone at Walker & Company; to Jean Doumanian, Patrick Daly, and Kim Jose at Jean Doumanian Productions; to Susan Glasier of the Lily Dale Assembly offices; to the Reverend Donna Riegel and members of her beginning mediumship class in Lily Dale; to Mark and Morgan Staub for their literary expertise and creative feedback; and to Brody Staub, just because he's Brody.

PROLOGUE

Monday, September 3
Erie, Pennsylvania
11:42 p.m.

She realizes, the moment she reaches the dark street and pats the back pocket of her jeans, that she doesn't have her cell phone.

Great.

What's she supposed to do now? Go back and look for it?

She turns and looks back at the house. Towering, with turrets, the three-story brick mansion might once have been beautiful. Now occupied by students at nearby Gannon University, the old home's doors and windows gape wide open, spilling stray people and loud music into the crisp September night. With a new semester just under way—and a party in full swing—there are cars on the lawn and bikes on the porch.

No way am I going back in there.

Not after someone figured out she's just a high school student and informed the hosts, who quickly—and loudly—kicked her out.

Talk about humiliating.

Why am I even here?

She usually doesn't go sneaking around behind her parents' backs, crashing college parties, but her friend Maria—who's still somewhere inside, flirting with some guy—talked her into it.

Now she's going to wonder where I am.

Well, too bad. She's not about to go back in to look for Maria. *Or* the phone, which she probably didn't even have with her in the first place. Or even her jacket, which she definitely *did* have with her and left draped over a chair inside.

Summer's definitely over, she thinks, wishing she had the jacket now. Shivering in her skimpy pink ribbed tank top, she checks her silver bracelet watch.

It's almost midnight. The original plan was for her to call her dad to come pick her and Maria up at the pizza-and-wings place around the corner, which is where they're supposedly hanging out after a movie on this last summer night before they start their senior year.

No phone, no jacket, no Maria . . . now what?

Her parents are going to kill her if she misses her curfew. They've been really touchy lately. They totally freaked last week when she bleached her reddish hair blond, right before she had her picture taken with the cheerleading squad for the back-to-school issue of the local paper.

You'd think she had pierced her tongue or gotten a tattoo

or something, the way Mom and Dad carried on. If they ever find out she was at a college party . . .

You'd better start walking, she tells herself firmly, tossing her newly blond hair.

Heading away from the lit-up party house, down the dark, deserted, unfamiliar street, she tries not to think about any of the horror movies she's seen. Naturally, they are all she can think about. Every tree, every parked car, seems to conceal a lurking ax murderer or fiery-eyed demon.

Stop it. You are such *a loser.*

She turns a corner, and then another. The night is deadly still. Her pink rubber flip-flops make a hollow slapping sound on the concrete sidewalk.

Something else reaches her ears, then: an approaching car. She hears it coming before she sees the headlights swing onto the block.

It seems to slow down as it comes closer, catching her in its bright spotlight with nowhere to hide. Already jittery, she now feels borderline frantic. She walks faster, heart racing.

The car is creeping now, coming up right alongside her. She hears the whir of an electric window being lowered, and a perfectly ordinary-sounding masculine voice calls, "Excuse me, miss? You shouldn't be out here alone right now. Miss?"

Holding her breath, she turns reluctantly toward the car. A man is behind the wheel.

Her mother always said never talk to strangers, but what is she supposed to do? Ignore him? Anyway, she's a safe distance away. It's not like he can pull her into the car from there. She can always run and scream bloody murder if he tries.

She can't make out his features in the dark, but she sees

3

him reaching into his pocket. Her stomach lurches. Is he going to pull out a gun and force her into the car?

She's about to take off when she sees something glint—and realizes it's not a gun at all.

It's a badge.

Oh. Thank goodness. Her knees go weak with relief. He's a cop.

"We had an attempted rape over on French Street. The perp took off running in this direction. You haven't seen him, have you? Tall guy, over six feet, with dark hair, about two-ten, two-twenty pounds, wearing a dark jacket and cap."

"No. I haven't seen him." She looks around fearfully, half expecting the hulking suspect to jump out from behind the nearest shrub and attack.

"Okay, thanks." The detective starts to roll up the window. "Just be careful, okay?" he calls, then adds, "You don't have far to go, do you?"

"I . . . uh, I was going to walk home, but it's up off of East Twelfth." And actual escaped rapists are way scarier than imaginary ax murderers and fiery-eyed demons. "Do you have a phone I can borrow to call my parents for a ride?"

"I do, but what are you going to do after you call? Wait around alone out here for them to come and get you? You'll be a sitting duck." He leans over and opens the passenger's-side door with a sigh. "Get in. I'll take you home."

He doesn't sound thrilled about it, but she hurries gratefully toward the car.

She settles into the seat. The car is warm. Good. That feels much better. If he hadn't come along, who knows what might have happened to her alone out here?

4

The detective rolls up the window and locks her door from the control on the driver's side.

"There," he says. "Safe and sound, right?"

"Right. Thanks."

"What's your name?" he asks as the car picks up speed.

"It's Erin."

"Hi, Erin. I'm Phil."

Phil? That's odd. Shouldn't he be calling himself Detective Something?

He comes to a light and stops the car. When it changes, he turns the corner.

Oops. "Um . . . Detective?" She can't bring herself to call him by his first name. "East Twelfth is that way."

He says nothing, just keeps driving as if she hadn't spoken. Maybe he didn't hear her.

"Excuse me? I live back that way," she repeats, and an uneasy feeling begins to creep over her again.

Still, he ignores her. He goes around another corner, again heading in the wrong direction, taking the turn so fast the tires screech.

Should a police officer be driving so recklessly? And shouldn't he know his way around? And shouldn't he be listening to her when she tells him he's going the wrong way?

"You know what? I need to get out," she blurts, stark fear transforming her voice into a little girl's, high pitched and vulnerable. "Please. Let me out."

She realizes that a faint smile is playing at the corners of his mouth. No. Not a smile at all.

A smirk.

He lied, she realizes in a burst of sheer panic. He isn't a detective at all.

And the danger wasn't out there on the street . . . it's right here in the car with him.

And I should have listened to Mom. Never talk to strangers.

Terrified, she begins to pray.

ONE

Lily Dale, New York
Tuesday, September 4
3:19 a.m.

With a trembling hand, eyes still blinking in the sudden glare from the overhead bulb, Calla Delaney turns on the tap at the pedestal sink in the upstairs bathroom. A deafening groan of Victorian-era plumbing sends a rush of water that seems to roar through the old cottage.

Oops—too loud. Calla hurriedly turns it off, not wanting to wake her grandmother. Standing absolutely still, breath caught in her throat, she listens for stirring down the hall.

Nothing.

Right. Odelia Lauder really does—as she likes to say—sleep like the dead.

Talks to them, too, Calla thinks with a glimmer of irony

7

despite the lingering dread still wrapped around her like a clammy towel.

Her grandmother is a medium—and she's not the only one.

Here in Lily Dale, Victorian cottages with hand-painted signs announcing psychic mediums in residence are as common as glittering neon casinos on the Las Vegas Strip.

Calla had no idea what she was walking into when she first flew to western New York State from Tampa a few weeks ago to visit the grandmother she hadn't seen in over a decade.

Who ever heard of a town dedicating itself to spiritualism for well over a century?

Okay, plenty of people have *heard* of it. That's obvious from the crowds of grieving visitors who wander up and down the streets every day, hoping to connect with their dearly departed.

But Calla was clueless about Lily Dale's genuine ghost-town status at first. And when she found out, she decided Odelia, and Lily Dale and everyone in it, was . . . well, some kind of freak.

Seriously, who in their right mind would actually choose to *live* in a place like this?

Calla's mom hadn't. The moment she was eighteen, Stephanie Lauder Delaney left Lily Dale and never looked back. Nor did she ever tell Calla about her hometown's eerie little secret.

No, I had to find that out on my own—the hard way.

A chill breeze off nearby Cassadaga Lake isn't all that crept over Calla as the overcast days of August wound to a close last week.

Yeah, things have changed pretty drastically since she got here. She now finds herself not only believing in Odelia and the others—and in ghosts—but regularly seeing and hearing them herself.

In other words, Calla seems to be, like her grandmother, spiritually gifted.

It sure has taken her long enough to suspect that Aiyana, the exotic-looking woman with the dark hair; Kaitlyn, the troubled, pretty teenaged girl; and the other strangers who pop in and out of her world these days might actually be . . . um . . . *dead*.

Psychic awareness is supposedly a hereditary gift, like the dreamy absentmindedness she inherited from Dad, or the slim-hipped, long-waisted build and delicate features she inherited from Mom.

I got this from her, too.

Slowly, she looks down and unclenches her left fist.

Lying in her palm, bathed in the yellow glow from the antique fixture above the sink, is the emerald bracelet Mom gave Calla when her boyfriend, Kevin, dumped her back in April.

"It's yours to keep," Mom said, hugging her. "I know it's just jewelry. It won't heal a broken heart, but it might make you feel better."

It did.

Until the clasp suddenly broke as Calla leaned over her mother's open grave in July. The bracelet fell from her wrist and was swallowed into the gaping hole where Stephanie's coffin had just been lowered.

Helpless, Calla knew it was lost to her forever—just as Mom was.

To her utter shock, she was dead wrong.

About the bracelet, anyway.

A few minutes ago, at precisely 3:17 a.m., in her mother's old bedroom across the hall, she experienced the impossible.

Mom's old jewelry box opened all by itself, playing the hauntingly familiar melody Calla has been trying to place from the moment she arrived here.

As it woke her from a deep sleep, she finally recalled where she'd heard it before.

And now that I remember—and now that this has happened—I'm really scared.

Calla looks down at the bracelet in her hand.

When she had jumped out of bed, there it was, lying in the open jewelry box.

The same jewelry box she had rummaged through many times since she arrived, as part of her mission to get to know the girl who had grown up here in Lily Dale and gone on to become Calla's mother.

The bracelet hadn't been in the jewelry box until now.

And I never really knew you at all, she silently tells her mother . . . wherever she is.

Suddenly the woman who raised her for seventeen years seems like a stranger.

With a shudder, Calla abruptly reaches for the tap and turns it.

Again, the groan of old pipes; again, the deafening splashing sound.

This time, though, she's hearing only the voices in her head. Mom's and Odelia's, repeating a long-ago argument that keeps echoing through Calla's mind when she's asleep. She was having the disturbing dream yet again just minutes ago, before the jewelry box opened itself and interrupted those eerie, chilling words that drove her mother and grandmother apart forever.

"... *because I promised I'd never tell* . . ." That was Mom, distraught, tearful.

"... *for your own good* . . ." That was Odelia.

"... *how you can live with yourself* . . ." Odelia again.

And then: "*The only way we'll learn the truth is to dredge the lake.*"

Calla doesn't know which of them said that. The voice was so shrill and desperate she couldn't tell.

But they had to be talking about the lake here—Cassadaga Lake, she thinks as she fits the rubber plug into the drain and watches the water fill the basin.

Just last week, Odelia sternly—and inexplicably—warned her never to venture into its cold waters.

Calla turns off the tap and drops the bracelet into the filled basin. A cloud of mud swirls around it, rapidly turning the water murky, then opaque, obscuring the bracelet as it sinks to the bottom.

Just like whatever dark secret lies at the bottom of Cassadaga Lake, waiting to be dredged up . . .

So that the truth can be told at last.

Calla wonders, as an icy ripple of dread flows through her veins, if she really wants to know what that is.

Staring at her reflection in the mirror, she gradually becomes aware that something is changing in the room. There's a sudden heaviness in the chilly night air.

On the tile wall behind her, the light casts tall shadows.

11

Human shadows. *Shadows.*

Two.

Two shadows?

But . . . how can that be?

Eyes wide, Calla stares into the mirror at the pair of distinct human forms on the wall behind her. One is unmistakably hers, frozen in fear. The other—almost the same height and size—is just beside it, as it would be if someone were standing right next to her.

But no one is there.

No one she can see, anyway.

Oh my God. Oh my God.

Is it a trick of the light? Or . . .

Is something here? *Someone?* Some presence?

Calla raises her left arm slowly and watches as one of the reflected shadows—her own—simultaneously does the same on the wall behind her.

The other shadow simply hovers there, motionless.

But it is there. Calla isn't alone.

She turns her head abruptly to the left, to the right, spins around completely.

The second shadow remains . . . but the small bathroom is otherwise empty.

Heart racing, she reaches for the dangling light chain above the sink and pulls it. The room is instantly plunged into darkness.

She counts to ten, then yanks the chain again.

Blinking in the sudden blast of light, she can see that the second shadow is now gone . . . and with it, the sense of a presence in the room.

12

She takes a deep breath to steady her nerves. It's only then that she notices the faint fragrance of lilies of the valley, Mom's favorite flower, hovering in the air.

"Mom," she whispers, shaken, "was that you?"

But of course, there's no reply. The presence is gone and she's alone again . . . or so it seems.

For now.

TWO

Tuesday had been a strange, cool, and stormy day. Calla spent most of it lying on her bed, wrapped in an old patchwork quilt handmade from her mother's childhood dresses, and brooding about all that had happened the night before.

She still doesn't know what to make of her mother's emerald bracelet reappearing.

She had tucked it back into the jewelry box, then checked all day to make sure it was really there, just in case she had imagined the whole thing.

Nope. It was definitely there when she fell into bed before eight o'clock, so physically and emotionally exhausted that she drifted right to sleep without even worrying about starting a new school today.

14

And it was still there this morning, when, for a change, Calla woke up well rested, having finally slept soundly through the night.

Now the air is fragrant with bacon, and she can hear pans clattering in the kitchen as she creaks slowly down the steep stairs. She left the bracelet behind. The clasp is probably still loose, and she doesn't dare risk losing it again.

Yeah, that, and you're still too spooked to wear it again.

Dressed in jeans and a long-sleeved black top from the Gap, she's toting her heavy backpack, bulging with school supplies her grandmother picked up for her. Her iPod is tucked into one of the pockets, just in case she finds herself with some downtime.

Missing is her cell phone. She never left the house without it back in Florida, but there's no need to carry it around now; she can't even get a signal here in Lily Dale.

Nor can she get online to check her e-mail, IM with her friends, maintain her MySpace page, write in her blog, surf the Web . . .

To do anything on the Internet, she has to go next door to use Odelia's neighbors' computer. Luckily, the girl who lives there, Evangeline Taggart, is her age and has fast become a good friend to Calla. The computer belongs to her aunt Ramona, who's raising the orphaned Evangeline and her brother, Mason, but she said Calla's welcome to come use it anytime.

Still, it's not the same. In her old life, Calla was used to being plugged into the world around her. Well, maybe not the world immediately around her . . . but, electronically, to the world beyond her family's doorstep.

Here in Lily Dale, she can be in tune only with her immediate surroundings.

Maybe, she's starting to realize, that's made her more sensitive to . . .

Well, a new kind of energy, which has nothing to do with electronics.

Even now, as she reaches the shadowy front hall, a sound reaches her ears: steady rapping.

She looks around, half expecting to see another inexplicable shadow . . . or perhaps a manifestation of Miriam, the resident ghost, who lived in this house a hundred years ago. She likes to make things go bump, not just in the night, but all day long.

Nope, no Miriam. This time, the rapping sound is coming from somewhere outside.

Calla glances out the window and immediately spots the very human source. One of Odelia's neighbors across Cottage Row is using a hammer to nail a sheet of weather-proofing plastic over the windows of his little house.

Farther down the street, a pair of heavyset women in plaid flannel shirts load boxes into the SUV parked in front of another cottage that's already been boarded up.

Wow. People are leaving town in droves.

The official Lily Dale "season" just ended on Labor Day weekend. According to Evangeline Taggart, the place empties out as most of the resident mediums head for warmer climates to avoid the harsh western New York winter.

They sure don't waste any time, Calla thinks, watching a car towing a U-Haul trailer rumble past.

Beyond the lofty trees and Victorian rooftops of the little

houses across the way, the sky is heavy with rain clouds. Cool air gusts through the screened window. Shivering, Calla pulls it down a little. Her thin Florida blood isn't used to weather like this—not in September, anyway. Her grandmother mentioned that the first snowflakes start to fall around mid-October, and the wintry weather doesn't fully let up until May.

Not that it matters, because Calla expects to be out in California with her dad by the time the real snow accumulates and winter gets under way. Which is kind of a shame, because she's seen snow only once in her life, on a family ski trip to Utah.

Leaving the chilly air and the misty gray view behind, she heads into the kitchen, where the overhead light dispels the gloom.

She remembers seeing the room for the first time a couple of weeks ago and comparing it to her Florida home's sleek, modern, expensive granite-and-stainless-steel kitchen with custom cabinetry.

Here, the floors are green-and-white linoleum and the walls are papered in an ivy pattern, peeling at the seams. There are white metal cabinets with metal handle pulls, an outdated olive green fridge and stove, and pale green countertops crammed with everything anyone could ever need in a kitchen, and cluttered with a lot of stuff nobody but Odelia could possibly ever need anywhere.

Today, the room—like the rest of the house—seems charming. Homey. Familiar.

"Happy first day of school!" Standing at the stove, Odelia looks up from the griddle where she's frying . . . something.

It doesn't look like eggs, or pancakes. It pretty much looks like . . .

"Mush." That came from Odelia.

"Mush?" Calla echoes.

Odelia lifts the corner of the griddle and points at the yellowy goo. "Fried cornmeal mush. Ever had it?"

"Nope." And she isn't particularly anxious to try it.

"Really? I'm surprised. It's a real southern thing. I'd think growing up down there . . ."

"Yeah, well." Calla shrugs. "I guess we've never eaten much Southern food. Maybe since Mom is—*was*—from here, and Dad is from Chicago . . . I don't know."

"Well, then, you've been missing out." Odelia slides a spatula beneath one of the blobs and expertly flips it. "There's nothing like starting the school day with a stick-to-your-ribs breakfast like fried mush and a side of bacon. I've got some under the broiler."

"I always just had cereal at home." Organic, unsweetened cereal. "Mom's pretty much a health nut. I mean . . . she *was*."

Will she ever get used to speaking of her mother in the past tense?

"Not when she was a kid, she wasn't." Odelia snorts and shakes her unnaturally red head. "She always could eat everything I put in front of her, and then some."

Her grandmother's back is to Calla. Her voice grows wistful, and her hand trembles a little on the spatula handle as she continues, "Back then, Stephanie loved everything that was bad for you. Her favorite was homemade fried chicken with mashed potatoes. She liked them with a whole lot of salt and butter and heavy cream. She'd pull up a chair to the counter and stand on it, and I'd let her do the mashing."

There's a long pause. Calla pictures a younger, thinner

Odelia standing at the counter, and Mom standing beside her on a chair, a little girl in pigtails, just like in the framed photo on the living room wall.

Odelia's back straightens and she swipes a hand at her eye, seeming to get hold of her emotions as she turns toward Calla. "If I do say so myself, I make the best fried chicken, mashed potatoes, and gravy you'll find north of the Mason-Dixon line."

"I bet you do, Gammy."

Odelia's a good cook, even if her taste buds are a little wacky. The night Calla arrived, she was taken aback to find that her grandmother put raisins in the meatballs and sugar in the spaghetti sauce. Turned out, it tasted pretty good.

She's getting used to Odelia's eccentric style in the kitchen. And in everything else.

Like her wardrobe. Today, her grandmother's plus-sized figure is crammed into leopard-print leggings and a yellowy orange fleece pullover. On her feet: a pair of beat-up purple rubber Crocs.

"So tell me," Odelia says. "Are you nervous?"

"Me?" Calla busies herself taking a carton of orange juice from the fridge. "Nervous?"

"You," Odelia agrees, looking at Calla over the pinkish cat's-eye glasses propped on the tip of her nose. "Nervous."

"Maybe a little."

"I would be. Maybe a lot. Starting a new school and all."

It's hard to imagine Odelia nervous about anything. She pretty much takes in stride everything from her semiperma-nent seventeen-year-old houseguest to Miriam and the other shadowy entities who hover around the house.

19

"At least you know a few of the kids already, though," Odelia points out.

Some better than others, Calla thinks, and a faint smile curves the lips Blue Slayton kissed after their first date last week.

Then she remembers Willow York, Blue's ex-girlfriend, and her smile fades.

Evangeline mentioned that Lily Dale High is pretty small. Meaning, Calla's bound to run into Willow there. On the upside, she's bound to run into Blue, too—along with Jacy Bly, who held the unofficial title of resident newcomer before Calla came along.

With Native American blood and exotic dark good looks, Jacy captivated her from the second she saw him. He lives down Cottage Row with two foster dads who took him in after Social Services took him away from his alcoholic, abusive parents.

He briefly told Calla about that when they spent an afternoon fishing together in Cassadaga Lake. But even after spending a few hours alone together, she found herself with more questions than answers about Jacy and his difficult past. She'd love to get to know him better—if that's even possible. Sometimes she sees him from afar, jogging past Odelia's house with a couple of other boys. He mentioned he's on the school track team.

Other than that, he seems to keep to himself.

But I can be that way, too, Calla thinks as she pours juice into a glass. She probably has more in common with Jacy than she does with the more confident Blue—who, come to think of it, hasn't called her since their date. He was supposed to spend last weekend in New York City with his father, the celebrity medium David Slayton, who was doing some television appearances there.

But he must have been back long before now.

Oh, well. It's not like Calla's hoping to get hot and heavy with Blue.

Well, maybe she was hoping it a little, after that amazing kiss.

Still . . . a lot has happened since then.

Including a visit from her ex-boyfriend Kevin, who drove up from Tampa and dropped his sister, Lisa—Calla's best friend—in Lily Dale last weekend. Seeing him again brought it all back: the exhilaration of her first love, and the heartache of being dumped for a college girl.

Kevin stayed only a few hours before heading on to Cornell—and, no doubt, his new girlfriend, Annie.

Monday night, Lisa flew back home to Tampa.

Calla was originally supposed to leave this week, too, headed to California, where she would have been starting school today. Dad, who is a science professor, is there on sabbatical, teaching at a university near Los Angeles.

At this point, he's still camping out on a friend's couch in Long Beach. He hasn't had much luck finding an affordable apartment for the two of them in a good public school district. Money's been tight without Mom's salary, and it turned out she didn't have a life-insurance policy.

Why would she? Who would have ever thought something could happen to Mom? She was so young, so together, so alive, so . . . needed.

Calla forces saliva past a hard lump in her throat and pushes away the painful thought.

21

Anyway, Dad seemed . . . well, not happy, but maybe a little relieved when Calla asked to stay in Lily Dale for a couple of months and attend school here. That would buy him more time to find them a place to live.

Of course, he doesn't know about Lily Dale's spiritual connection. If he did, no way would he have agreed to let Calla stay—or, for that matter, to have come here in the first place.

He can't find out, no matter what. I have to stay—at least until I figure out what's going on.

Her knees a little wobbly, she sinks into a chair at the table. Sipping her orange juice, Calla makes a face at its wateriness. Back in Florida, it was always freshly squeezed and thick with tangy-sweet pulp.

Florida.

Not *home.*

When did she stop thinking of Florida as home?

Is this creaky little cottage in this spooky little town her home now?

No. Not really. But it was Mom's home for eighteen years, and Calla feels closer to her here than she would anywhere else at this point.

Sure, she's had occasional flashes of homesickness for Tampa. But she couldn't stand living in the house where Mom died, and she isn't anxious to go back . . . maybe not ever.

How can she face going up and down those stairs every day? The bloodstains at their foot were scrubbed away with bleach . . . but the memory of those horrible red splotches on white tile can never be wiped from Calla's mind.

Calla closes her eyes, remembering her mother's crumpled body, wearing an elegant charcoal gray suit with round, shiny black buttons. She remembers the unnatural angle of Mom's neck, the frozen look of horror in her gaping eyes . . .

The official ruling was accidental death. Mom, in a pair of high-heeled black Gucci pumps she often wore, had tripped and fallen down the stairs.

Mom, who had never made a careless mistake in her life . . .

Until she burned the Irish soda bread on Saint Patrick's Day after the stranger calling himself Tom—who wasn't a stranger at all—showed up at the door.

The telephone rings abruptly and Calla is lifted, gratefully, from those grim thoughts.

"Can you pick it up?" her grandmother asks, busy at the stove. "It might be your dad, calling to wish you luck on your first day."

Calla doubts that. It's barely four a.m. in California.

"Hello?"

"Calla? It's me!"

"Lisa?" Her friend's familiar drawl is a welcome sound. "What's up?"

"You are. And so am I, unfortunately." Lisa yawns loudly in her ear as Calla steps into the next room with the phone, away from her grandmother's perked-up ears. Odelia can be pretty nosy. Even nosier than Mom.

"What are you doing calling me this early?"

"Being a good friend. Today's your first day, right? I thought you might be stressing and I figured I should call and tell you it's going to go great."

"How do you know?"

"I'm psychic."

23

Calla can just see Lisa's sly grin. "Well, that makes one of us, because I have no idea what to expect. I wish . . ."

She trails off wistfully.

"I know," Lisa says somberly. "I wish the same thing. But hang in there. You'll be okay."

"You really think so?"

"Yup. It'll be fun to meet new people. Here I am, stuck with the same old faces we've seen since kindergarten."

Calla wants to tell her she'd trade places in a second, but a wave of homesickness clogs her throat.

They chat for a few more minutes, and she tells Lisa to say hello to all her old friends and teachers.

"I'll tell them you'll be back to visit soon," Lisa promises.

"How am I going to do that?"

"I have a comp airline voucher you can use. They handed them out when my flight was delayed because of the storm the other night."

"Don't you want to use it yourself?"

"Nah. If I want to fly up north again, my parents can pay," Lisa says with a laugh.

Calla smiles, knowing the Wilsons would be more than willing. Kevin always did say they spoil his sister.

Her smile fades when she remembers that Tampa is no longer home, and nothing there is the same. Not without Mom and Dad.

"Thanks for the offer," Calla tells her, and swallows hard. "For now, I've just got to focus on getting through this day."

"I know. Good luck. Love you."

"You too."

She hangs up and returns to the kitchen.

"Good timing. Here you go." Odelia bustles over to set a heaping plate on the table, along with maple syrup and butter. "Dig in."

Calla swallows hard. "I . . . I'm not really that hungry."

"Eat anyway. It'll calm down those first-day-of-school butterflies in your stomach. Trust me."

If only the first day of school were the only thing I had to worry about.

With a sigh, Calla reaches for a fork.

The redbrick school building is outside the actual town, beyond the wrought-iron gate with its sign that welcomes people to LILY DALE ASSEMBLY . . . WORLD'S LARGEST CENTER FOR THE RELIGION OF SPIRITUALISM.

Evangeline Taggart joins Calla for the ten-minute walk down the winding country road along the lake's grassy shore. Her younger brother, Mason, lags behind them with a couple of his friends. Calla can see a couple of other kids with backpacks up ahead, also headed toward the school.

As they walk along, Evangeline chatters away as usual. Her hazel eyes dance as she tells Calla about shopping for school clothes yesterday at the Galleria in Buffalo with her aunt, who thought she should start dressing up more for school now that she's getting older.

"I didn't listen, in case you didn't notice," Evangeline says with a laugh, and gestures at her sneakers and simple long-sleeved blue T-shirt, untucked over her jeans to help camouflage her well-padded hips and thighs. Her slightly frizzy reddish hair is tamed more than usual, though, held back with a silver barrette. And she's wearing lip gloss.

"So what's it like not to have to wear a uniform to school for a change?" Evangeline asks.

"I don't know yet . . . I used to complain about it, but maybe in some ways a uniform was easier. You never have to think about what to wear."

"Well, if you're worried, don't be. You look fine."

"The thing is, I'm going to run out of stuff to wear in, like, two days," Calla tells Evangeline. "I didn't come up here thinking I was going to stay past summer."

"If you want to go shopping for warmer clothes," Evangeline tells her, "I'll go with you. That would be fun. We can go to the mall and you can get some sweaters and a down coat. What do you think?"

"Yeah, that would be good," Calla murmurs, realizing there's just one problem with that scenario: she's broke.

Money wasn't a problem when Mom was alive. She gave Calla a generous allowance and they often went shopping together. Mom loved to buy clothes for her. Now, even if Calla found her way to a mall, it's not like she could buy anything. And it's not like she feels comfortable asking her grandmother for money, or even Dad, for that matter.

Having faced far more traumatic problems these last few months than a wardrobe that's seriously lacking, she puts the matter out of her head.

At least she looks halfway decent today, and that's what counts.

She took the time to brush on mascara and rim her hazel eyes with a smudged liner pencil. She worked gel into her long, sun-streaked brown hair before she dried it, to make it look thicker and help keep her bangs out of her face. She's overdue for a haircut, and the bangs are starting to bug her.

Disturbed as she's been about what's been going on around here, she didn't overlook the fact that she's going to be seeing— and be seen by—both Blue Slayton and Jacy Bly today.

"Hey, I meant to ask . . . how did your visit go this weekend? With your friend Lisa?"

Hearing the wistful note in Evangeline's voice, Calla wishes she had thought to invite her over.

Then again, maybe it was better that she didn't introduce her newest friend to her oldest. They couldn't be more opposite: honey-blond, overprotected Lisa, with her designer wardrobe and her healthy skepticism for all things Lily Dale–related, and down-to-earth, orphaned Evangeline, with her disdain for fashion and her extracurricular classes in subjects like Crystal Healing and Past-Life Regression.

Oil and water, Calla thinks, and is glad she kept her two friends apart. At least, this time.

"It was fun," she tells Evangeline. "But the weekend flew by."

"You must miss her, huh? How long have you guys been friends?"

"Since kindergarten."

All at once, the breeze off the lake seems to grow cooler. Goose bumps spring up on Calla's arms, and she hurriedly slips into her fleece-lined Windbreaker, glad she thought to grab it.

"I've known most of the kids in my class since kindergarten, too," Evangeline is saying, idly kicking a stone along the road. "But my best friend, Amy, moved away last year after her parents split up. The two of us used to do everything together. Now I just kind of hang with whoever's around."

"Like me?" Calla flashes a teasing smile.

"Yeah, right. Oh, before I forget to ask . . . do you ever do any babysitting?"

"Sometimes I did, back home. Why?" Calla shivers a little and decides she really is going to need warmer clothes around here.

"This friend of my aunt's, Paula, just broke her ankle, and she needs help after school for a few weeks with her kids. They're really cute, two and five. I can't do it because between my schoolwork and extracurricular stuff and another babysitting job I've got, I'm booked. But I told Paula I'd ask you."

Caught off guard, Calla automatically hedges. "Oh . . . well, I'm not sure . . ."

Then again, what else has she got to do?

And—hello—you were just worrying about being broke, remember?

Now she's suddenly got the opportunity to earn some cash. *Anyway, being around cute little kids might be good for you,* she tells herself, realizing she's feeling oddly—and quite suddenly—gloomy.

"You should do it," Evangeline is urging. "Paula's great. You'll like her a lot. And she pays great. Why don't I just give her your number so she can call you and talk to you about it?"

"Whatever, go ahead," Calla agrees, distracted by the plunging temperature and the strange oppression that seems to have drifted into the air.

Then she catches movement out of the corner of her eye and notices, with a start, that she and Evangeline aren't quite alone.

For a split second, she wonders if the girl with the long blond hair is someone Evangeline knows from school.

Oh. Whoa. There's a filmy quality about the girl's slender build.

Is she . . . ?

Yes. She's an apparition.

It's happening again, and Calla's skin tingles as she notes the mounting sensation of thickening in the icy air.

The girl turns her head abruptly to meet her gaze, and Calla recognizes her instantly.

Kaitlyn Riggs.

THREE

The first time Calla glimpsed her a few weeks ago, Kaitlyn Riggs was with her mother, Elaine, who had come to Odelia for a reading.

When she spotted Kaitlyn in Odelia's kitchen, Calla had no idea the girl wasn't alive—or that for some reason, Calla alone could see her.

Calla caught sight of her again just last week on a MISSING poster and immediately understood the reason behind Elaine Riggs's repeated missions to Lily Dale.

Her daughter had been abducted from an Ohio shopping mall, and Elaine was desperate to find her.

New to the world of psychic mediums—and even newer to her own spiritual gifts—Calla didn't immediately understand the clues Kaitlyn's spirit was conveying to her. When she finally pieced it all together, she called Elaine Riggs and told her that the search should be focused on a specific area of a remote state park.

Monday night, the woman turned up on Odelia's doorstep to tearfully thank Calla for bringing closure, even if it wasn't the happy ending she had hoped for.

Her daughter's strangled body had been found in the exact spot where Calla had redirected the search to.

Odelia was livid. The moment Elaine left, she laid into Calla.

Kaitlyn Riggs was murdered, Calla. And you were given information about her case. The way you chose to share it with her mother . . . well, I know your intentions were good, but I wish you'd come to me first. It takes years to learn how to deal sensitively with people who are grieving. Sometimes it's still hard for me, and I've been at this forever. But what I'm most concerned about is that you could have gotten yourself hurt . . . Kaitlyn's killer is still out there somewhere.

Remembering her grandmother's ominous words—and seeing Kaitlyn again now—sends a shudder of dread through Calla.

Why is Kaitlyn back?

She's gesturing with her hands. She seems to be trying to communicate something, and Calla senses that it isn't mere gratitude.

Evangeline seems oblivious to the ghostly presence, the accompanying chill, and Calla's distraction. She's chattering on about the unpopular menu in the school cafeteria.

Frustrated, looking into Kaitlyn's wide, troubled blue eyes, Calla asks, "What? What is it?"

"Sloppy Joe? You mean you've never heard of it? Lucky you!" Evangeline exclaims, obviously thinking Calla's been following the conversation. "It's ground beef—supposedly—all mixed up in some kind of sauce that's sticky and red and hideous."

Sticky.

Red.

Hideous.

Calla shakes her head to fight off the image those words are about to bring to mind.

Beside her, Kaitlyn Riggs is wide-eyed, nodding slowly, meaningfully.

What? What are you trying to tell me?

Upset, Calla closes her eyes to shut out both Kaitlyn and the rush of familiar bloody memory that's sweeping over her.

Or is it familiar after all?

No. Not this time. Because that's not her mother's battered, facedown corpse Calla is seeing in her mind's eye.

It's a stranger's.

And the body's not lying on white ceramic tile. No, it's outside somewhere. Dirt . . . pinecones . . . a few golden maple leaves. There's a cluster of bowling-ball-sized rocks near one of the dead girl's bare feet, laid out in a circle.

She's got long blond hair, like Kaitlyn. It's matted with twigs and leaves.

She's slightly built, also like Kaitlyn. Her arms—thickly covered in strawberry-orange freckles—are bare and dirty and scratched. There's a silver bracelet watch on one wrist, caked in mud. She's wearing jeans and a pale pink shirt . . . and it's spattered in blood.

Disturbed by the harsh image, Calla opens her eyes abruptly. Evangeline is still talking about cafeteria food, still oblivious. Yes, and Kaitlyn is still here.

As Calla looks at her, she gives a satisfied nod.

That's her.

The two words drift into Calla's head. They came from Kaitlyn. She's certain of that, though she isn't sure if she actually spoke to Calla or just planted the thought in her mind.

That's her? Calla echoes silently. *Who? The bloody girl in pink?*

Again, Kaitlyn nods.

"What about her?" Calla blurts, frustrated.

Evangeline breaks off in midsentence and gestures. "You mean Willow?"

"Yes. No!" Following Evangeline's gaze at a slender dark-haired girl walking up ahead, she realizes it's Blue Slayton's ex-girlfriend. "I didn't even realize she was there."

"But I just pointed her out to you." Evangeline frowns . . . then the frown fades and the light seems to dawn. "You're not talking about Willow. You're not even talking to *me* . . . are you?"

Slowly, Calla shakes her head. Why deny it? Maybe it'll be a relief to tell someone other than Odelia about her new-found gift. Or curse.

"No, I was talking to her," she admits to Evangeline. She waves a hand in the air as she turns toward Kaitlyn again, daring to hope that Evangeline might be able to see her too. After all, she said herself that she has psychic medium abilities, just like her aunt Ramona and her late parents.

But it's too late to find out whether Evangeline can also see the apparition.

Because Kaitlyn is no longer visible, even to Calla. The spot where she stood is empty, the chill gone, the air noticeably thinner.

"You were talking to who?" Evangeline wants to know.

"Um . . . to . . ." Belatedly, Calla remembers that her grandmother told her not to mention her ability to anyone. She said it the other night, after Elaine Riggs had left.

"Spirit?" Evangeline asks almost cheerfully, and snaps her gum.

Calla shrugs, numb.

Evangeline apparently takes that as a confirmation. "I knew it!"

"You knew what?"

"That you've got psychic awareness. I sensed it."

She sensed it. Right. Because she, too, has the gift. The curse.

So it's not like I told her, Calla argues mentally with her grandmother. *She guessed.*

Yeah, and Odelia should know there's not a whole lot a person can get away with here in Lily Dale.

Evangeline's next comment catches Calla off guard.

"You know, your grandmother used to think you might be destined for this. I heard her tell my aunt that once, a long time ago."

"How long could it have been?" Calla asks, frowning. After all, she's only been here a few weeks. But the way Evangeline said it, it sounded as if she meant . . .

"Oh, years ago."

"*Years?* You mean . . . my grandmother thought I was a medium before she even knew me?"

34

"Of course she knew you. She just hadn't seen you since you were really little."

Wondering how much Evangeline—and her aunt, for that matter—have heard about the falling out between Mom and Odelia, Calla muses, almost to herself, "Why would she have thought that about me?"

Evangeline supplies the answer unexpectedly, and knowingly. "Because she was there when you were born, and she said there was a caul over your face. That's a fetal membrane—in case you didn't know."

Calla didn't know. About any of this. "What's it for? The caul?"

"They say babies who are born with one will be sensitives. Odelia had a caul when she was born. So did Aunt Ramona."

"How about you?"

Evangeline shrugs a little defensively. "I don't know. I mean, I was born in some hospital. I bet no one was paying attention. I'm sure I had one. Anyway, your grandmother definitely saw that you had a caul, and she told my aunt that she never mentioned it to your mother because she didn't want to upset her."

"So Mom didn't know?"

"I guess not. Maybe she was too out of it. Or, well, Odelia always said your mother wasn't interested in . . ."

"Spiritualism?" Calla supplies when Evangeline trails off. "Psychic powers? Talking to ghosts? What?"

"Any of it, I guess. She didn't believe in any of it. That bothered your grandmother. So anyway, even if your mother had known you had the caul, she probably wouldn't have told you or done anything about it."

"Like what? What could she have done?"

"Like brought you here, or taught you how to use your gift, or whatever."

No, Calla thinks, *she definitely wouldn't have.* Mom never mentioned that her hometown was a spiritualist community or that her mother was a medium. She obviously wanted to leave that life behind.

And now here I am, in the thick of it. What would Mom think about this?

"The thing is, Calla . . ." Evangeline seems hesitant.

"What?"

"You need to be careful. With what you can do, and with how you use it. That kind of power can be dangerous."

"How?"

"So many ways. Registered spiritualist mediums go through years of training to learn how to use their abilities responsibly."

This is the second time she's been warned about this, and Calla can't help but feel as though both Evangeline and her grandmother are being overly dramatic.

"I'm not sure I get what you're saying," she tells Evangeline, trying not to sound skeptical.

"I'm saying it's important to use your gift for the greater good, and to learn how to protect yourself when you open yourself up to the Other Side. You have to remember, you're being used by spirit energy as a medium. You're conducting the energy . . . whatever kind you let come through. If you don't learn to pray and protect yourself from the negative energy . . ." She trails off ominously.

Calla can't help but shudder. "You're scaring me, Evangeline."

"I don't mean to. But, look, why don't you come to a beginning mediumship workshop with me? I mean, you're in Lily Dale—what better place to educate yourself?"

"I don't think I'm ready for something like that," Calla tells her.

"It's not that big a deal. It's basically a message circle."

"No, thanks."

She knows that message circles are like seances. Some are open—meaning anyone can participate—and some are closed because, as her grandmother explained, an experienced group of mediums are working together regularly and using their collective energy to channel spirit guides and messages.

"Let me know when you change your mind," Evangeline tells Calla.

Not *if* you change your mind. But *when*. As if she fully expects that Calla will decide to put her sixth sense to use now that she's figured out she has it.

Everything happens for a reason. Mom herself always used to say that.

If that's true, Calla's coming to Lily Dale is no accident.

And Mom's death might not be, either.

Maybe one even has something to do with the other.

As for the most recent visit from Kaitlyn Riggs, and Calla's disturbing vision of the bloodied girl in pink . . .

It all means something.

She just has to figure out what it is . . . and what she's supposed to do about it.

The corridor smells of hot food as Calla makes her way toward the cafeteria after social studies, her fourth-period class.

So far, so good. Things are going better than she expected, being the new kid for the first time since kindergarten. Wait, kindergarten doesn't even count, because everyone else is new too.

Here, everyone else gives off the comfortable, easygoing attitude that comes with familiar territory.

This was familiar territory for Mom by the time she started her senior year here. Just knowing that this is where her mother went to school gave Calla chills when she first walked up the broad stone front steps.

Not *you're about to see a ghost* chills. More like *if you're not careful, you're going to burst out crying in front of everyone* chills.

Calla quickly discovered that beyond the old-fashioned redbrick exterior of Lily Dale High are equally old-fashioned green chalkboards, banks of gray metal lockers, scuffed hardwood floors, and straight rows of desks.

This place is a world away from Shoreside Day School back in Tampa, with its state-of-the-art labs, indoor-outdoor classrooms, and lecture halls housed in a sprawling cluster of sleek, modern buildings that feel more like a college campus than a high school.

Here, she's found her way to every classroom with little trouble—not all that hard, considering that the two-story school has simple L-shaped hallways on both floors. She's been assigned a homeroom and a locker, memorized her combination, and accumulated a stack of textbooks. She's even seen a few familiar faces: Lena Hoffman, who works at the Lily Dale Café, has the locker next to Calla's, and Willow York, of all people, has turned up in most of her classes so far.

When they found themselves sitting across the aisle from each other in health class first thing this morning, Willow acknowledged Calla with a brief smile, which totally caught her off guard.

Not that she expected Willow to stick out her tongue, but still. As Blue Slayton's barely ex-girlfriend, Willow can't be thrilled that he's gone out with someone else. And Evangeline told Calla that Willow knows all about that. "Lily Dale is smaller than any small town you'll ever see," Evangeline said cheerfully. "Everyone knows everything about everyone."

Right. And sometimes even before it happens.

Well, Willow has class, Calla has decided. She's not going to make a big deal out of Calla seeing Blue. Good for her.

And even better for me.

Pausing in the doorway of the cafeteria, Calla lingers to read the posted menu. Sloppy Joes today, like Evangeline predicted.

She reads the menu intently, checking to see what's on it for the next few days. Then next week.

Then, when she can't stall any longer, she forces herself to walk into the cafeteria.

This is what she's been dreading all day: the prospect of eating alone. Unfortunately her one friend, Evangeline, isn't here. When they compared schedules in the hall after homeroom, they found that their paths cross only once a day: in gym.

As Calla crosses the threshold into the cafeteria, her heart sinks. Instead of the small round tables that fill the cafeteria back at Shoreside, there are long rectangular tables. Most of them are filled with people who have known each other since kindergarten. It's going to be impossible for her to duck over to a secluded table alone and hide.

Is lunch even mandatory here? She definitely isn't hungry, thanks to Odelia force-feeding her mush and bacon. She's about to flee when she hears someone call her name.

Looking up, she sees Blue Slayton beckoning from a table filled with guys.

Hmm. Maybe she'll stick around. She walks over, tossing her head a little to get her hair out of her face without being obvious.

"How's it going?" Blue asks when she arrives at his side.

"Great," she says, noticing that he's wearing a long-sleeved jersey in a deep indigo shade that matches his eyes—and his name.

He wears that color a lot, she's noticed, and she's sure it's no accident. He has to be aware of the striking impact. And his clothes are expensive. She can tell by the cotton fabric that looks as thick and soft as his light brown hair, which he might wear in a wavy and slightly unkempt style, but she knows that's no ten-dollar barbershop haircut.

No, everything about Blue Slayton is expertly and deliberately pulled together. The result is effortless good looks that take her breath away a little every time she sees him up close.

"So you haven't gotten lost yet?" he asks Calla, fork poised above a tray that holds two of everything: two sloppy joe plate lunches, two bottles of juice, two ice cream bars.

"Not yet." She wonders if he's going to eat all that himself, or if he's planning to share with someone else. Willow, maybe?

"The only way to get lost around here is trying to find your way home if a blizzard blows in during the day," comments the red-haired, freckled guy sitting next to Blue.

"Yeah, but that only happens, like, once a week in the winter, and so far, we've lost less than a dozen kids that way," Blue says dryly, and everyone laughs.

He introduces Calla to the redhead—Jeremy—and to the other four guys, two of whom are named Ryan. They're all on the school soccer team together.

"Calla's living over in the Dale with her grandmother," Blue tells them, and a couple of them ask her politely about where she's from and how she likes it here.

As she answers their questions, she wishes Blue would invite her to sit down, but he doesn't.

Well, that's probably because he's with all these guys.

Or maybe it's because he's no longer interested in you.

"Hey, Calla," he says abruptly, "want to go out Friday night?"

Or maybe he is interested.

"Sure," she hears herself say as her heart trips over itself. "That would be great."

"Good. I'll call you." Blue drains what's left of his open juice and crushes the plastic bottle in his fist before reaching for the second one.

She takes that as her cue to leave.

But Blue Slayton asking her out again is enough to ease the humiliation, five minutes later, of roaming the room with a full tray, looking for a seat that has empty chairs around it. She doesn't want to just go and plop herself down next to anyone. That would feel kind of . . . bold.

But none of the open chairs has a buffer zone around it, and she can feel people looking up at her as she passes their tables.

She just has to sit down somewhere. Anywhere.

She looks around and her gaze falls on a striking girl with long black hair, porcelain skin, and a familiar face. Willow York again, and she glances up from a conversation she's having with the girl next to her. "Oh, hi."

"Hi." Calla hesitates, still holding her tray.

"Want to sit with us?" asks the other girl, who is African American, with a short, chic haircut, gorgeous dark eyes, and a mouthful of braces. She points to the empty chair across from her and Willow.

"Definitely." Calla gratefully puts her tray on the table and slips into the chair without stopping to see if Willow seems to want her there.

"This is Sarita," Willow says, in a friendly enough tone, "and you and I have already met. A few times, right? But I'm Willow . . . in case you forgot."

She didn't forget.

"Do you live in Lily Dale?" Sarita asks.

"Yeah, I'm staying with my grandmother." Calla decides not to tell her it's only temporary. Why complicate the conversation? "How about you?"

"I live down the road in Cassadaga."

Does the fact that Sarita lives outside the Dale mean she can't see dead people or have psychic visions or premonitions?

What about Willow? She lives in the Dale. Is she a medium?

Even more important: did Willow see Calla talking to Blue a few minutes ago? Probably not. She's acting pretty friendly.

Or maybe she's over him.

Nah. Remembering Blue's piercing eyes—and those broad shoulders beneath the soft cotton jersey—Calla can't help but think it would take any girl a long time to get over him.

Including you, she warns herself. *So don't go letting yourself get hooked on him.*

Yeah. One broken heart per year is more than enough.

Hearing a commotion, she looks over to see that someone just tripped and dropped his lunch tray. Her first thought: *Thank God that didn't happen to me.*

Her next: *That poor kid.*

He's enormously obese, with jet black hair, thick glasses, and a line of fuzz on his upper lip.

A few kids are laughing as, flustered, he wipes red sauce off his hands and starts to pick up the mess.

"Oh, no, poor Donald." Willow is instantly up and out of her seat, hurrying toward him.

"That's Donald Reamer," Sarita comments to Calla. "He's the kind of guy who . . . well, you know. Things are hard for him."

Calla nods. She does know. There was a Donald Reamer at her school in Florida, too—only it was a girl, and her name was Tangie Alvin.

Surprised at Willow's compassion, she watches her hand him a pile of napkins before stooping to salvage what's edible from his dropped lunch. She can see that a group of girls at a table next to them are snickering and rolling their eyes.

After a cafeteria aide has appeared with a mop and bucket and Donald has lumbered on his way, Willow goes over to the table of girls and says something to them. Their smirks vanish and they immediately look uncomfortable.

Willow returns to the table and reclaims her chair without comment. Sarita seems to be taking the whole thing in stride, saying only, "I hope they give him another lunch without charging him."

"Me, too. So . . . what'd you think of Kiley?" Willow asks Calla conversationally, and bites into an apple. Calla notices her tray contains only that, a small container of yogurt, and a bottle of water. Sarita's holds the same.

"Kiley?" For a second, she's blank. Then, "Oh! You mean the health teacher? She seemed nice."

Willow and Sarita exchange a look.

"Yeah, she puts up a good front . . . on the first day. They all do. Just wait. Have you had math yet?"

"It's last period."

"Then you probably have Bombeck, with Willow. He's famous for being hard-core," Sarita says. "My sister was straight A's until she landed in his class. She still talks about him, and she graduated four years ago. My mom even had him and said he was really hard even back then. He's been here forever."

"Well, hopefully I'll be okay." Calla picks up her fork, trying not to wonder whether her own mom might have had Bombeck, and whether she went to school with Sarita's mom. "I usually do pretty well in math."

Straight A's, actually. She's been an honor-roll student all the way through high school, but she doesn't mention that. She doesn't want to sound like she's bragging.

"Math is my strongest subject," Willow tells her. "And even I'm worried. You don't know Bombeck."

"I'm so glad I didn't get him for math," Sarita says contentedly.

"So you have Davidson, right? And who do you have for English?" Willow asks.

As Sarita pulls her schedule out of her backpack to compare it to Willow's, Calla toys with her fork. She's reluctant to dig into her steaming, hearty sloppy joe lunch in front of the other girls. She should have gotten fruit, yogurt, and water, like they did. She wants to fit in.

Then again . . .

Mom was always telling her not to follow the crowd. *Who cares what the other girls are eating?* her mother's voice asks in her head. *Who cares what they think of you?*

I kind of do, Mom. Just this once. Calla closes her eyes, barely aware of Sarita and Willow, who are chatting about a mutual friend. *I can't help it, Mom. I want to fit in here because . . . well, I don't fit in anywhere else anymore.*

Don't worry, you will, her mother's voice says, and she can hear it so clearly in her head that she wonders if her mother is actually here.

Focus. Maybe if you really focus, you'll be able to see her.

She tunes out all the background noise, thinking about her mother. About how desperately she misses her.

Please. Please, Mom. If you're here, let me see you. Please.

Gradually, Calla becomes aware of a strong presence. Someone is watching her. She can feel it.

She braces herself, opens her eyes, and looks up, expecting to see a shadow or even her mother's ghost. Or . . . Kaitlyn's.

Please let it be Mom this time. Please . . .

FOUR

It isn't her mother.

It isn't even a ghost.

Instead, Calla locks eyes with Jacy Bly, sitting one table away and looking intently right at her. He doesn't jerk his dark gaze away, the way another guy might if he were caught in the act of staring.

No, Jacy just nods a little, as if he's saying hello.

Calla nods, too. Just slightly. *Hello right back.*

Trembling—feeling almost like they've just had physical contact—she looks down at her untouched plate of food. Across from her, Willow and Sarita are absorbed in comparing their new class schedules.

Maybe Calla should be disappointed that the person she sensed wasn't her mother. Instead, she finds her heart beating a little faster at the knowledge that Jacy was looking at her as though . . .

He's interested. Definitely.

Great, but . . .

What about Evangeline? She has a thing for Jacy. She's always talking about him.

But it's not like they're dating or anything, Calla reminds herself. *And it's not like Jacy's going to ask me out, either, like Blue did. Twice.*

Jacy's too shy.

So there's no need to feel guilty about Evangeline.

Yet, anyway.

Ten minutes and one uneaten lunch later, Calla finds Jacy falling into step beside her as she exits the cafeteria behind Willow and Sarita.

She sneaks another peek at him. His short black hair is spiky on top, as though he rubbed a towel over it after a shower and walked out the door. Tall, lean, and muscular, he's wearing worn jeans, sneakers, and a plain white T-shirt. He probably threw them on without thinking about it, as casual about his appearance as Blue Slayton is deliberate. But the end result is the same. Jacy, too, is so good-looking he takes her breath away as she looks up at him.

"Are you glad you're here?" he asks her quietly.

"Yeah. I am. Are you?" He looks taken aback, and she realizes what he thinks she meant. Her face grows hot and she blurts, "I mean, are you glad *you're* here! Not, you know, are you glad *I'm* here. Because you wouldn't be. I mean, you wouldn't think about it. I mean . . . uh, are you glad you're here?"

He flashes her a slow grin. "I've been here a while."

What is it about Jacy that makes Calla shove her foot into her mouth every single time she opens it?

"But do you like it here?" she asks, and he shrugs.

"Things happen here that don't happen anywhere else. Or, didn't. Not to me."

Her heart beats faster. "Me, too. Things happen to me here, too."

"I know."

"What?" She stares at him. "How do you—"

"Hi, guys!" Without warning, Evangeline pops up in their path. *Who-what-when-where-why?*

"Huh?" Calla asks, and Evangeline laughs.

"You know . . . what did I miss? Anything interesting that you're talking about?"

If she only knew.

"Just school," Jacy says. "In other words, not interesting."

Calla wishes her friend hadn't interrupted this particular conversation, but she smiles at Evangeline as if she's glad to see her.

"Are you guys coming from lunch?" Evangeline asks, and her voice is a little higher pitched than usual, her smile so bright—and stiff—that she's baring most of her teeth. She gets so nervous around Jacy, and it shows.

"Yeah, it was sloppy joes," Calla tells Evangeline. "Like you said."

"I knew it!"

Calla considers making a lame joke about her friend's psychic powers but decides against it. Instead, she asks, "How about you? Are you going to lunch?"

That question is about as unnecessary as Evangeline's was, since the cafeteria is all that's on this end of the building. But for some reason, she has this need to keep the conversation going and stick to mundane topics. Topics that have nothing to do with the fact that Evangeline just stumbled across her and Jacy together.

"Yup. I'm going to lunch. But I'm not eating sloppy joes, that's for sure." Calla doesn't miss the way Evangeline checks out Jacy, then runs a hand quickly through her hair to straighten it.

Nor does she miss the way Jacy doesn't seem to notice.

That's because he's not even looking at Evangeline. He's looking at Calla.

"See you in math later," he says. "We're in that class together."

"How do you know that?"

He just offers a cryptic smile before waving to both her and Evangeline and striding off down the hall.

"Did you eat lunch with him?" Evangeline immediately asks Calla.

"No!" Oops . . . did that sound too defensive? Softening her tone, she adds, "I ate with a couple of girls. Willow and, um, Sarita."

"Oh, Sarita's great." Evangeline relaxes a little. "And Willow can be really nice, when she wants to. She's just moody. So everything's going okay, then? You're finding your way around?"

"Yeah. And"—she leans closer to Evangeline to whisper—"Blue Slayton just asked me out again!"

"No way! Are you serious? That's great!" Pause, then, "So Willow knows that and she still ate lunch with you?"

"Oh . . . uh, no, she doesn't know that. But . . . they're broken up, right?"

"Supposedly. Anyway, who cares? I'm so psyched for you,

Calla. I mean, anyone in this school would kill to go out with Blue, and you waltz in here—the new girl—and he's all over you."

Calla smiles at the exaggeration and tries not to wonder if Evangeline's crush on Jacy is part of the reason she's so enthusiastic about Calla's involvement with Blue.

If she hadn't come along just now, where would the conversation with Jacy have led?

Does he know about me seeing dead people? Calla wonders. *Can he see them too?*

Maybe he can help her make sense of everything. The bracelet, the lake, the dreams about Mom and Odelia, and the strange, gory vision Kaitlyn Riggs just showed her.

She has to talk to Jacy again, first chance she gets.

"Hey . . . there's my girl. How was school today?"

"Hi, Dad! It went really well," Calla replies into the phone, swept by a sudden wave of homesickness at the sound of Jeff Delaney's voice, just as she was by Lisa's this morning.

She sinks into a chair at her grandmother's kitchen table, glad Odelia is busy in the closed-off sunroom at the back of the house, doing a reading for a client. Suddenly, she longs for some time alone with her father, even if it is just over the phone.

"Did you make any new friends, Cal?"

"A few," she says, thinking of Willow and Sarita. In gym class this afternoon, Evangeline introduced her to a girl named Kasey, who was a captain and chose Calla second for her team when she was sure she'd be the last one picked.

And then, of course, Jacy Bly was in her last period, math, with the dreaded Mr. Bombeck. He seemed strict and he ran a tight ship. To Calla's disappointment, she didn't get a chance to talk to Jacy during class, other than a brief hello.

Later, she spotted him up ahead when she and Evangeline were walking home toward Lily Dale, but she wasn't about to call out to him. Not when her friend had just said, dreamily, "Ooh, look, there's Jacy. I would so give my right eyeball to go out with him."

"I've already been getting to know a few kids who live near Gammy," Calla tells her father now, "so it was good to see some familiar faces around."

"I'm glad it went well."

"Oh, and guess what? I just talked to this lady who broke her ankle and needs a babysitter for a few weeks. So I told her I'd do it."

Ramona's friend Paula wasted no time calling this afternoon. Calla liked her so much over the phone that she agreed to take the job without meeting her or the kids in person. She starts tomorrow after school.

"That's great!" her father says, but his voice sounds a little hollow.

He's lonely, she realizes. *He sounds as homesick as I feel.*

Terrific. Now she's getting choked up. Fighting tears, she reaches for the glass of iced tea Odelia had waiting for her when she walked in the door, along with a plate of oatmeal cookies warm from the oven, and a message from Lisa, who had called twice wanting to know how her day went.

She takes a big gulp of the tea, hoping to wash down the lump that threatens to clog her throat.

"Gammy, huh?" her father says quietly on the other end of the line.

For a moment, she's confused. Then, after retracing the conversational path, she explains, "It's what I used to call her . . . when I was really little." Okay, now she feels uncomfortable and she's not even sure why.

"I know that. I remember. I just haven't heard it in a lot of years."

Calla is silent for a moment, then finds herself blurting, "Dad, what happened between the two of them? Mom and . . . Gammy. Why did they drift apart?"

"Drift apart?" He snorts. "They were both forces to be reckoned with, Calla. There was no drifting where those two were concerned. It was more like a violent earthquake ripped a huge, gaping chasm between them."

"So they had an argument, right? Because I kind of remember it."

"They had a lot of arguments. They never got along very well—but don't let that change how you feel about your grandmother," he adds hastily. "She's definitely headstrong and eccentric, and I can't say I ever really understood where she was coming from. But she's a good person. And like I said, your mother could be difficult, too."

It's the first time since Mom's death that she's heard her father say anything less than complimentary about her.

Looking back on their marriage, Calla knows it worked for them, but now she can see that her mother was in charge, and her father either went along with her or made himself scarce. Not always physically. Sometimes he just buried his head in a book or his research.

For the first time, Calla wonders if there was more than just ordinary tension between her parents. She never paid much attention. Never had a reason to.

Until she figured out the real identity of the stranger who visited Mom on Saint Patrick's Day.

"I know Mom and Gammy didn't get along," she tells her father, "but there was one big argument that caused the rift, right, Dad? Because . . . I mean, I was there. I remember it."

Silence.

"Dad?"

Calla decides his cell phone must have broken the connection and is about to hang up when her father asks quietly, "What do you remember?"

Oh. He's still there. Well, he's always been the kind of person who gets lost in thought, prone to long silences. That's why it isn't easy to carry on a long-distance father-daughter relationship. She needs to see him.

Longing, suddenly, to be face-to-face with him, she asks, "Dad, what do you mean, what do I remember?"

"Do you remember anything about that fight? Because your mother never told me what it was about. She wouldn't talk about it. All I knew was that I got home from work one night and your grandmother had left with all her luggage, and never said good-bye. I never talked to her again until I called to tell her . . . about Mom."

His voice cracks, and the aching lump again threatens to strangle Calla.

She longs to tell her father what she fears more than anything: that her mother's death wasn't an accident after all. But that would mean telling him about that man, the one who

53

visited on Saint Patrick's Day and called himself Tom—not his real name—and distracted Mom so that she burned the soda bread. If Calla closes her eyes, she can still see him standing at the front door, holding a manila envelope. He was whistling that strange tune, looking as though he wanted to appear totally casual.

Calla spotted him again in the crowd of mourners at Mom's funeral in July.

That was the last she saw of him . . . until she got to Lily Dale. But her latest sighting wasn't in person. No, he's pictured in a framed photo on Mom's dresser.

He's her high school boyfriend. Darrin Yates.

Calla didn't recognize him until the night the jewelry box opened by itself and she found the bracelet.

She knows now that his recent connection to Mom was about more than just old friends catching up. It had to be. Otherwise, wouldn't he have introduced himself when Calla answered the door? Wouldn't Mom have been happy to see him? Wouldn't she have told Calla about their old times together after he left, instead of being so remote and upset? Definitely upset.

Ramona Taggart had known both Calla's mother and Darrin. She said he was troubled, and that Odelia disapproved of her daughter's relationship with him. Darrin disappeared not long before Mom left Lily Dale and was never heard from again.

Not by anyone here, anyway.

Mom obviously heard from him . . . not long before her unexpected death.

Okay, so what did he want?

And what was in the envelope?

I have to find out. It's important.

Calla is certain of that. The message she's being given by Aiyana—or whatever spirit is communicating with her—has something to do with Darrin's connection to Mom.

Maybe even something to do with . . .

Mom's death?

I have to tell Dad about this, Calla decides . . . just as a chill drifts into the room.

Shivering, she realizes she isn't alone. She looks around, expecting to see an apparition.

The kitchen is empty.

But the presence is as real as the goose bumps prickling the back of her neck.

Aiyana, Calla finds herself thinking.

It's her. She's here.

She doesn't know how she knows that. She just does. She can feel her.

And she doesn't want me to tell Dad about Darrin. Because he doesn't know. Mom kept it a secret.

Calla isn't sure how she knows that; the thought seems to have been placed in her mind by the invisible presence.

"Calla," Dad says, "you should know that your grandmother loved you. And your mother, too. Whatever happened . . . well, it was a terrible shame. All those lost years."

"So Mom really never spoke to Gammy again?"

"Not that I know of. She was really upset. What did they argue about? Do you remember? Because at the time it didn't seem that important, but lately . . ."

When he trails off, Calla prods him, "What, Dad? Lately, what?"

"I don't know. There are just some things . . . your mom—" He cuts himself off. "I shouldn't even be talking about this with you. And none of it matters anyway. I was just curious if you remembered what your mom and Odelia argued about."

The only way we'll learn the truth is to dredge the lake.

Should she tell him?

No. Aiyana doesn't want her to say anything. Calla senses that somehow.

Anyway, his grief is as raw as her own; he doesn't need to dwell on anything even more painful than losing his wife in an accidental fall.

"I don't really remember," she tells him, with only a faint prickle of guilt. It's for his own good. She has to protect him. At least, for now.

Her father sighs heavily. "Yeah, well, like I said, it doesn't matter. Anyway . . . the real reason for this call—aside from seeing how you did in your new school today—is that Jet Blue is running a weekend fare sale. I can fly to New York City and connect. What do you think about that?"

"You mean . . . connect to *here*?"

He laughs. "Well, Buffalo. That's close enough. I need to hug my girl."

His girl.

He used to call Calla and her mother his *girls*.

Now I'm all he has. And he's all I have.

Well . . . she has Odelia, too.

Odelia—Gammy—does love her.

And she did love Mom. That's obvious. No matter what happened between them, Odelia loved her.

56

So what on earth happened to drive mother and daughter apart?

Why don't you just ask?

This time, the thought didn't come from Aiyana.

No, Calla realizes, the presence—and the chill—have evaporated.

So . . .

Why *doesn't* she just ask her grandmother what happened?

Maybe I will, she tells herself. Meanwhile . . .

"I'd love to see you, Dad," she hears herself say before it occurs to her that she just made a terrible mistake.

If her father comes to Lily Dale, he's going to realize what goes on around here and haul her back to California with him on the next plane out.

"I know how busy you are, though," she adds hastily, "and I'll be out there soon enough, so I don't want to make you spend all that money just to—"

"Calla, this is costing me less than two hundred bucks round-trip and I've already got my ticket. I'll be there Friday."

"Next Friday?" Okay, that'll give her only a week to figure things out, but—

"No," he says, sounding pleased with himself, "this Friday. Day after tomorrow."

FIVE

Thursday, September 6
7:55 a.m.

"Oh, before I forget to tell you," Evangeline says as they walk into school the next morning under surprisingly warm sunshine, "I can't walk home with you today. I have to stay after."

"For what?" Calla asks, running a hand through her bangs and wishing she could get a haircut.

"There's a meeting for anyone who plans to run for student council officer. Hey, want to come?"

Calla smiles at the invitation. "Considering I've gone to this school for, like, twenty-four hours and I'm not even staying the whole year, probably not a great idea. Anyway, I'm going over to Paula's to babysit, remember? But I promise I'll vote for you."

"Thanks. I really want to win, because if you're an officer

senior year, you're an officer forever. You know . . . you get honored at the reunions and everything. My dad was class president when he went to school here."

That makes Calla wonder about her own mom, and her smile fades.

As she and Evangeline part ways and she heads toward her locker, she thinks about how little she knows about what her mother was like in high school. Not just the stuff involving Darrin. But all of it. Like whether Mom was a class officer, and whether she ever had Mr. Bombeck for math.

It's not earth-shattering information. Just everyday details. The kind you barely notice when they come up in conversation with someone.

Just like you never go around thinking that every conversation you have with someone could be your last, so you better pay attention, and get everything said.

Now I'll never know about Mom in high school. Unless . . .

She can always ask Gammy. Or Ramona.

But that's not the same.

And nothing ever will be, she reminds herself glumly, *so you'd better get used to it.*

"Calla! How's it going?"

She turns to see Blue standing there, looking hotter than hot, as usual. He's wearing a blue-and-red hooded Buffalo Bills sweatshirt, and his backpack is slung casually over one shoulder.

"Oh, hi. Listen, I have to tell you something," she blurts, trying to gather her scrambled thoughts.

"Yeah? What's that?"

"I can't go out tomorrow night after all because my dad is coming to visit."

"Yeah?" Looking completely unfazed, he asks, "How about next Saturday night then? I've got a soccer game on Friday, so . . ."

"Next Saturday? Uh . . . sure! Definitely."

"Great. See you later, okay?"

"Sure." Calla turns back to her locker, smiling as she twirls the combination lock.

She'll have to remember to call Lisa back later and fill her in about school—and Blue.

So far, she's off to a pretty good start, just as Lisa, the so-called psychic, predicted.

For the second day in a row, Calla stands in the cafeteria with a tray, looking around for a place to sit.

Only this time, she bought only a yogurt and a container of grapes instead of the hot lunch—baked macaroni and cheese. That smelled and looked good, but Odelia stuffed Calla full of zucchini frittata for breakfast, and she's not that hungry.

There's Blue, sitting with the same group of guys. She hesitates, wondering if she should go over there and talk to him.

Seeing him throw back his head and laugh at something one of the Ryans says, she decides not to approach him now. She'd feel too self-conscious with all the other guys there.

Not that she doesn't feel pretty self-conscious anyway, just standing here alone with her tray.

She looks around for Jacy, thinking maybe she'll work up the nerve to go over and talk to him about the stuff that's been happening to her here. There's no sign of him, but Sarita has spotted her and is waving her over. She's sitting at a table in the far corner with a girl who has her back to Calla, but she can tell it's Willow by the gorgeous mane of dark, shiny hair.

Relieved and grateful, Calla weaves her way toward them. Willow was in a few of her classes this morning, but they were kept so busy there was no time to talk. Unlike Calla's school back in Florida, there's no coasting into academics as the school year gets under way. Here, *bang*—day two, and you're in the thick of it.

"Hi, want to eat with us?" Sarita asks, pulling out the empty chair beside her.

"Sure, thanks." She sits, and notices that Willow is awfully busy peeling an orange. She pulls off the last wedge of peel, then goes to work removing every thread of white membrane.

"How's everything going for you guys today?" Calla asks a little uneasily, and Sarita tells her everything is great. Willow looks up briefly, says, "Okay," and goes back to the orange.

There's a definite chill coming off her today that wasn't there yesterday.

She knows, Calla realizes. *She knows I'm seeing Blue again.*

For a moment, she's glad she didn't go over and talk to him just now. The last thing she needs is for Willow to spot them together.

Then she realizes that's ridiculous. Willow and Blue are broken up. He can talk to—and date—other girls if he wants to.

Yeah, but Willow doesn't have to be friends with those girls.

"So, what were you saying about that trip your parents are planning?" Willow asks Sarita as Calla unwraps her straw.

Sarita goes back to what she was saying before Calla arrived. It's a good thing she talks a lot, Calla decides by the time the lunch period is over, because there was no awkward silence, and there might have been. Sarita and Willow are both on the homecoming dance committee, and they're working on a flyer. Sarita at least asked Calla for some input—not that she had anything worthwhile to add—but Willow didn't say much to her at all.

It isn't that she's being particularly rude or cold-shouldering Calla. She seems more . . . detached. Or maybe even hurt. Sad.

She still cares about Blue, Calla realizes. *They might be broken up, but that probably wasn't her idea.*

Just like what happened with Kevin and me.

And if Calla found herself sharing a lunch table with his new girlfriend, Annie, she probably wouldn't be all that chatty, either.

Oh, well. What does any of this matter? She's not staying in Lily Dale forever. She'll be heading out to California soon enough for a fresh start.

Only . . .

She can't go until she's taken care of unfinished business here.

Again, she looks around for Jacy. He's not here.

That will have to wait.

"Calla?" Mr. Bombeck, who is wiry and middle-aged, with thick glasses and a swoop of graying hair, comes to a halt beside her desk. He looks over her shoulder at the pop quiz in front of her. "Is there a problem?"

Not unless you count the fact that I have absolutely no clue how to even set up the first problem, much less solve it.

The classroom is hushed; all around her, pencils are scratching and her classmates are intently focused on the quiz.

"It's only the second day of school. How can we have a test when we haven't learned anything yet?" someone protested when Mr. Bombeck sprang it on them.

The stern reply: "That's the point. I want to see where your math skills are."

Calla realized, a few seconds in, that hers seem to have vanished into thin air, the way things often do in Lily Dale.

She looks up at the teacher now, shrugs, and whispers, "I'm sorry . . . I just don't understand these problems."

He nods a little and crooks a finger at her, gesturing for her to come with him.

She hesitates, then pushes back her chair. It makes a loud scraping sound on the hardwood floor and the entire class looks up at her. Everyone except Jacy Bly, that is. He's intently focused on his test.

"I want you all to keep working," Mr. Bombeck announces. "I'll be right outside the door, and I'll be monitoring you through the window. Keep your eyes on your own work, please."

Calla follows him out of the classroom, her face burning.

Mr. Bombeck closes the door behind them and positions himself in front of the rectangular window so that he can keep watch on the classroom.

"I was afraid you might have trouble, Calla."

"No, but . . . I've always been good in math. Straight A's. I was supposed to be in Advanced Placement Calculus back in Florida." Sharing that with him doesn't feel like bragging.

Right. It's more like sheer desperation. She can't let the toughest teacher in her new school conclude she's ignorant.

"I'm sure you did well there, but you did come from out of state." He jerks the doorknob, pushes it open, and calls, "John, put all four chair legs on the floor." Without missing a beat, he closes the door and goes on to Calla, "Our math curriculum here is extremely challenging."

Yeah, no kidding.

"What should I do?" she asks helplessly.

"I'm going to assign you to a study partner for the next week or two. Let's see if we can get you caught up. You're staying with your grandmother in the Dale, right?"

When she nods, he says conclusively, "Willow York lives near you, and she's got a terrific track record in math. The two of you can start working together right away."

Willow York . . . again.

Could her life be any more complicated?

"Jacy! Wait up," Calla calls, spotting him in the hallway just after the last bell.

His long legs were about to carry him around the corner to the stairwell, but he turns and looks back at her.

He doesn't smile, but as she hurries toward him, she can't help but decide he seems glad to see her. Smiling—and flirting—just aren't his style.

"Can I talk to you for a second?" she asks him, watching

him swing his backpack over his shoulder after zipping his gray hooded sweatshirt.

"About math? Is everything okay?"

So he did notice that she had to leave the classroom with Bombeck. After their little talk, the teacher sent her to the school library for the remainder of the period. He said it made no sense for her to sit there while everyone else finished the test. She could feel them all watching her while she gathered up her things and left the classroom.

"Everything's okay with math," she tells Jacy, "I just need some extra help."

"I can help you if you want."

Yeah, I wish. If only Bombeck had assigned Jacy to be her study partner, instead of Willow. Maybe she can suggest that to—

No. She'd better not mess with Mr. Bombeck. He's been human enough so far, but she can tell there's a steely core underneath. Besides, he said he'd tell Willow to call her after school, so she must already know about being assigned as Calla's study partner. If Calla backs out now, Willow might think she doesn't want to work with her because of Blue.

Which is kind of true, she admits to herself.

"I was looking for you during lunch," she tells Jacy. "Where were you?"

"Outside. I took a walk in the woods."

"Really?" She checked the student handbook yesterday and found out the school has a closed lunch rule, meaning you have to stay in the cafeteria. Or so she thought. "So we're allowed to go outside, then? During lunch?"

"No." He shrugs. "What did you want to talk to me about?"

She looks around, not wanting anyone to see them together.

Anyone? You mean Evangeline.

"Calla?"

She likes the way Jacy says her name. Some people around here, with their Great Lakes accents, make the *a*'s flat and nasal, drawing it out into *Key-alla*.

Not Jacy.

Who, by the way, is still waiting for her to say something.

"Uh, sorry . . ." She tries to remember what it was she wanted to talk to him about.

Oh. Right. *That.*

Instantly, she's plunked right back down to grim reality.

"Yesterday you said something about my being gifted. Well, not in those words, exactly, but . . . you know what I mean."

He nods. "I know."

"Can we—" Again, she looks around to see who might be eavesdropping.

The hallway is filled with the sound of slamming lockers and chattering voices and people are scurrying around, not seeming to pay any attention to Calla and Jacy. Still . . .

"Are you . . . ," she begins again, and then, "I mean, do you want to . . . ?"

"I'll walk home with you. Yeah. Come on."

"Good thing you're a mind reader." She grins.

Again, he doesn't.

And this time, it occurs to her that it's because he doesn't think she's joking. Around here, it seems, some people don't take things like mind reading lightly.

Calla just hopes Jacy can't read *all* her thoughts. Especially the ones about him.

They head down the stairs and swing by her locker so she can get her stuff. As they step outside into an unexpectedly balmy breeze, Calla notices that the shifting sky is ominously dark in the west, beyond the lake, and wind-driven ripples cover the surface of the gray-black water.

"It's going to storm," she comments, reminded of Florida in the late afternoons.

Jacy shakes his head. "No. It'll pass."

"How do you know?"

He ignores the question and asks one of his own as they head down the path toward the road back to Lily Dale. "So what's been going on?"

"I don't even know where to start." She searches her memory. "I guess the first thing was the clock. This digital one that was in my room—my mother's old room. When I first got here, it was flashing."

"Because the time wasn't set?"

"Right. Exactly. I didn't bother to set it, but then I woke up in the middle of the night and it said 3:17 a.m."

"So, someone set it while you were sleeping?"

"My grandmother said she didn't. And it started happening every night. I'd go to bed with the clock flashing, and I'd wake up and it was 3:17. Every single night."

"Maybe you were dreaming."

"I wasn't," she says firmly. "Not about waking up. But I was definitely dreaming before I woke up. The same exact

67

dream, every night. It was about my mother and my grand-mother, and this argument they had when I was really little. After that, they never saw each other again."

"What was it about?"

"I don't know, really. They kept saying something about dredging the lake."

Both she and Jacy glance again at the dark water. What secrets does it hold?

Calla shudders and turns away, going on with her story. "I was starting to get really freaked out, so I unplugged the clock, and . . . this is the really creepy part . . . it happened even then."

"It was unplugged, and it was showing the time anyway?"

"3:17. Yeah. So I threw the clock away, and bought a new one, and . . ." She wonders how she's going to tell him this without sounding like she's really lost it.

But she doesn't have to, because he says it for her. Like he already knew.

"And it happened anyway."

"Yeah. And I found out that spirit energy can supposedly tap into appliances and, you know, manipulate electronic energy. Feed off of it or something."

It's Jacy's turn to nod. Obviously, this isn't news to him.

"The thing is . . . last weekend, when I was at Wal-Mart buying the new clock, this green shamrock bowl somehow fell off a shelf by itself and broke into a million pieces. And then I saw this woman again. This Spirit," she remembers to say, instead of *ghost*. Here in Lily Dale, people like to say Spirit. With a capital *S*. "I think she made the bowl break to get my

68

attention because . . ." She takes a deep breath. "This is going to sound far-fetched."

Jacy shrugs.

"Okay . . . green shamrock bowl. 3-17. That's not just a time, it's a date. March seventeenth. Saint Patrick's Day. That's what this was all about. I realized I was supposed to be remembering something that happened on Saint Patrick's Day. Does that make sense?"

"Yeah," Jacy says simply, and she wants to hug him. "What happened on March seventeenth?"

"This man came to visit my mom. I remember the day because she was baking Irish soda bread, and she burned it. She never made careless mistakes like that. She must have been thrown off by seeing him, or maybe something he said, or something he gave her—he had an envelope with him."

"What was in it?"

"I have no idea. I thought it must be work stuff, but it turned out he wasn't a coworker after all. And his name isn't really Tom, either. The other thing is, he was whistling this tune. I had never heard it before, but I heard it again, when I got to Lily Dale. It's the same song that plays in this old jewelry box I found in my mother's room."

Jacy's black eyebrows raise, just a little. He's not the kind of guy to react to anything in a big way, Calla's learning. But he looks surprised.

"And in the middle of the night last Monday—Tuesday morning, really—at 3:17—it opened by itself," she hurries on, "and the music woke me up, and I found my mother's emerald bracelet in there, and it couldn't have been there, because it fell into her grave at her funeral and I lost it." She breaks off, breathless, wondering if Jacy thinks she's crazy. Sometimes, lately, she thinks that herself.

"What about the woman you saw that day, when the bowl broke?" Jacy asks. "Who was she?"

"I have no idea. But this word—*Aiyana*—popped into my head when I saw her. Does that mean anything to you? Is it a name or something?"

"It can be. It's Native American. It means 'forever flowering.'"

Her jaw drops, and she remembers the distinct floral smell that sometimes inexplicably fills her room back at Odelia's house, and infiltrated the bathroom the other night, when she saw that strange disembodied shadow. The scent belongs to lilies of the valley. Mom's favorite flower.

"I think that's the woman's name," Calla tells Jacy. "She keeps popping up . . . even before I came to Lily Dale. And she looks beautiful and exotic, like you."

It takes her a second to realize she just told Jacy she thinks he's beautiful. Oops.

Open mouth, insert foot, once again.

Not that she doesn't have more important things to worry about right now.

She says hastily, "I mean, she looks like she might be Native American. Like you."

"Where have you seen her? Other than Wal-Mart, I mean."

"At my mother's funeral back in Florida was the first time. Only then, I thought she was real. I mean . . . alive. You know—not in Spirit. And I saw her a few times around my

70

grandmother's house, and by the lake. I think she's been trying to give me messages. About my mom."

He's quiet for a minute, just walking along beside her, like
he's lost in thought.

Then he asks, "Did you ever hear of a spirit guide?"

Calla nods. "Yeah. They're kind of like guardian angels.
Right?"

"Kind of," Jacy agrees.

"Do you think Aiyana is my spirit guide?"

"She may be."

"That's it." *I know it.*

He knows it, too, she thinks, watching Jacy bend to pick up
a pebble and then resume walking.

"Do you think I'm the only one who sees her?" she asks
him.

"Depends. Sometimes guides come through clairvoyant
vision, sometimes they actually materialize in human form, or
sometimes we can only hear or feel them. Sometimes they can
even be an animal, or a symbol."

"Do you have a spirit guide?"

"I have a lot of them. We all do. Everyone has them, but
not everyone can perceive them. Some are permanently with
us from the moment we enter the earth plane until we leave
it, and others come and go when we need them."

From the moment we enter the earth plane.

His phrasing strikes Calla as typical of the way people
speak here in Lily Dale. Most places, people would just say
from the moment we're born.

"Are your guides . . . men?" she asks him. "Women?
Boys? Animals? Symbols?"

71

"All of the above, depending on what kind of guidance I need. They show themselves to me as they want to be seen, based on where I'm at."

"What do you mean?"

He hesitates, as if he isn't quite willing to open up with personal information.

Sure enough, when he does speak, he turns the reference back to her.

"Like, with you, you just lost your mom, so maybe—and I don't know for sure—Aiyana represents maternal energy and that's why she appears to you in the form of a woman."

She considers that. It makes sense. And seems comforting, in some bizarre way.

"Spirit guides are here to protect us, right?" she asks Jacy.

"To guide us." Jacy is choosing his words carefully. "It's up to us to decide what to do, though. They aren't responsible for our choices. We are."

"Right. I read that somewhere. And it said—in this book I got from the library here—that if you need their help but aren't even aware that you do—or that they exist in the first place—they'll try to get your attention somehow. What I don't get is, how can they warn someone who doesn't even know they exist?"

"They'll try to make you aware, maybe try to warn you somehow if they think you're in danger, but it's up to you to be receptive and heed the warning."

"Do you think Aiyana is trying to warn me about something? Or maybe give me some kind of message?"

"What do you think?" Jacy bends his arm to toss the stone toward the lake.

Calla hesitates, watching it skip several times across the gray surface of the water.

If she lets Jacy in on her secret suspicion about her mother's death, there will be no going back.

Out on the lapping water, the stone disappears from sight and sinks into the murky depths.

"I think she wants me to know about something that has to do with my mother," Calla tells Jacy. "With how she died, or . . . was killed."

Jacy stops walking and looks at her.

Then he nods slowly.

He gets it, Calla thinks, and on the heels of that, *so maybe I'm right about Mom being murdered—and Darrin having something to do with it.*

Just inside the wrought-iron gate to Lily Dale, Jacy points at a two-story cottage similar to most of the others here, with an architectural style typical of the eighteenth century.

"That's where Paula lives," he tells Calla.

"Do you know her?"

"This is a small town. You get to know everyone, really fast."

"Oh. Well . . . thanks for walking with me, and for . . . listening."

He nods.

"Jacy," she says, as he turns to head toward home.

"Yeah?"

"What do you think? About all the stuff I told you." He was so quiet while she spoke, but she got the impression he was listening intently, and processing all of it.

"I'm not sure," he says slowly, tilting his head.

"But do you think there might be something to it?" Calla presses him. "Do you think Darrin had something to do with my mom's death?"

"I'm not sure. But we'll have to talk about it some other time. I've got to go get ready for track practice, and you're babysitting right now anyway."

What is there to say to that except, "Yeah, you're right. Thanks."

Resisting the urge to watch him walk on down the road, Calla turns back toward Paula's house.

"Hey, Calla?" she hears him call, and spins around. She finds him walking backward, gesturing at the sky, which is solidly blue again. "Told you the storm was going to pass."

She smiles. "Yeah, you're right, it did . . . this time."

But she has a feeling, as she turns back to Paula's house, that there will be plenty of other storms to come around here.

The front yard is overflowing with a riot of blooming flowers, and there are statues of garden gnomes, a little wishing well, a bird bath, a weather vane, and a wrought-iron stand holding a nylon banner dotted with brightly colored falling leaves and the words *Welcome Autumn*.

Back in Calla's Florida neighborhood, sprawling, modern homes were fronted by plain old grass, ornamental shrub borders, and maybe a tastefully placed palm tree or two. There was a definite less-is-more attitude where landscaping is concerned.

Here, it's obvious that more is more.

Paula's busy yard mirrors many others in the Dale, and Calla finds the overall effect strangely conflicting. Almost as if

74

all that over-the-top outdoor cheerfulness is supposed to off-set the genuinely haunted houses beyond—which, with their Victorian architecture and sometimes ramshackle state, actually tend to *look* like haunted houses.

This one is painted gray, with trim in various faded shades of green. Like many houses in the Dale, its roof slopes upward, then flattens off at the top—a mansard roof, Odelia calls it. It has old-fashioned scalloped shingles and a gingerbread porch with several spindles missing. There's a little red tricycle parked beside the door, and a shingle above it that reads MARTIN DRUMM, CLAIRVOYANT.

Calla climbs the steps and rings the bell.

Almost immediately, the door is thrown open by a little boy with white-blond hair and solemn eyes. "I'm Dylan," he announces. "You're Calla."

She smiles. "Right. Nice to meet you, Dylan."

He glances over his shoulder and murmurs something.

"I'm sorry, what did you say?"

He looks back at Calla. "Oh, I wasn't talking to you. I was talking to Kelly."

"Kelly?"

"That's his imaginary friend," a woman informs Calla as she hobbles into the hall on crutches behind the boy. "You know how kids are, right? Anyway . . . hi, I'm Paula."

She's heavyset but attractive, with short blond hair and a friendly smile.

Calla wonders about Dylan's imaginary friend. She does know how kids are. And anywhere else in the world, she'd assume an imaginary friend was just that.

Here in Lily Dale, however, she's not so sure.

"Can you believe I did this to myself?" Paula asks, gesturing at her bandaged right ankle. "I tripped over my younger son's toy fire truck and went flying. What a klutz. Come on in."

Stepping into the house, Calla can immediately see how that could have happened. There's stuff everywhere—toys underfoot and on every surface, along with the usual household clutter. A red-cheeked toddler with a headful of blond curls rolls into the living room on a scooter, calling, "Hi! Hi! Hi!"

"That's Ethan," Paula says. "He loves people."

She's not kidding. Ethan rolls right over to Calla's feet and throws his arms around her legs. "Hi!"

She laughs. "Hi, Ethan."

"So," Paula says, "what I basically need you to do is keep the kids busy so that I can try and start dinner and my husband can concentrate on his work upstairs. He's writing a book."

"Really? That's great." Out of the corner of her eye, she watches Dylan whisper something to an invisible companion.

"Yeah. It will be if he ever gets his research done. That's not easy with two little guys in the house, but he's plugging away. I figured you can take them out back to the picnic table since it's so nice out. Maybe play a game or something."

"Do you like to play games?" Dylan asks Calla, tugging on her arm.

"I love to play games."

"Did you ever play Candyland? It has my name in it on the box. D-Y-L-A-N. That's why I love it so much."

She grins. "Sure. I love Candyland, too, even though it doesn't have my name in it."

"Candyland!" Ethan echoes, clapping his chubby little hands.

76

And off Calla goes with them, relieved to have found a reprieve—at least a temporary one—from all that's been troubling her here in Lily Dale.

The sun-splashed afternoon with Paula's kids was so pleasant that Calla finds herself feeling almost lighthearted when she's back home at her grandmother's house.

Odelia has made a delicious eggplant lasagna. As they eat, Calla tells her about school and her afternoon babysitting, careful to leave out her walk home with Jacy. They're both polishing off their second helpings of lasagna when the phone rings.

"It's for you. Willow York," Odelia tells Calla, passing the receiver to her.

"Oh . . . hello? Willow?"

"Hi, Calla. Mr. Bombeck wants me to help you with the math. Are you available tonight?" She doesn't sound particularly friendly, but she's not unfriendly, either. More like . . . briskly efficient. Like someone taking a phone reservation from a stranger.

"I think so. We're eating right now, but I'll be finished soon."

"Okay. Can you come to my house at seven o'clock?"

"That's fine."

"Good. See you then."

She hangs up to find Odelia watching her, wearing a pleased expression. "I didn't know you were friendly with Willow. You're really creating quite the social circle around here, aren't you?"

Calla thinks about telling her it's just a study session. Then again, why burst Odelia's bubble?

After dinner, Odelia disappears behind closed doors with a newly widowed elderly client. The phone rings as Calla's washing the dishes.

Maybe it's Jacy, she thinks fleetingly, before dismissing that idea. He said they'd talk tomorrow.

It's probably just someone looking for a reading with her grandmother. Calla plucks her hands from the hot, greasy orange dishwater; rinses them quickly; and picks up the phone.

"Yes, hello. Calla Delaney, please?" The voice in her ear is male, formal, and asking for her.

Who can it be? Definitely not Jacy or Blue.

Why would a man be calling her?

Oh no . . . Dad!

What if something happened to him in California?

Please, no . . . no . . . don't do this to me. I can't bear it.

SIX

"This is Calla." Her voice trembles and she grips the counter with one hand to steady—and prepare—herself.

The lasagna roils in her stomach as she wonders if this is what the spirits were warning her about all along.

Is she an orphan?

"I'm from the AP in New York, calling about the Columbus Dispatch piece."

The Columbus Dispatch piece . . . the Columbus Dispatch piece . . .

The words are in English, but they might as well be in some exotic foreign tongue for all Calla comprehends. But the most important meaning is crystal clear: this isn't about her father. Not if this person is calling from New York . . . and the AP? That makes no sense whatsoever.

Unless he's calling to take back her AP math status. Can they do that? And so soon?

"I know I'm having a hard time in math, but it's only been two days—one, really—and I'm going to work with my study partner tonight, so I hope you'll give me a chance to stay in the program . . ." She trails off, deciding not to tack on a *pretty please?*

Maybe she should have, though, because the man is silent.

"Hello?" she says after a minute, wondering if he's hung up on her.

"Oh!" he says suddenly, and starts to chuckle. "AP. You thought I meant Advanced Placement program!"

"Didn't you?" she asks, confused—not to mention resenting the fact that he's laughing at her, even as she's relieved that whatever he's calling about, it's definitely not bad news about her father, because he wouldn't find the least bit of humor in that. "What are you talking about, then?"

He gives a little sigh the way people do after a good laugh, then says in a regular voice, "I'm from the Associated Press."

Like that makes any more sense than the Advanced Placement program.

"You must have the wrong number," she says, before remembering that he asked for her by name and . . . oh!

It's a newspaper: *Columbus Dispatch.*

As in Columbus, Ohio?

That's where Kaitlyn Riggs lived . . . and not far from where her murdered body was found the other day . . .

Thanks to me.

"I'd like to speak to you about your role in the Riggs case," the man tells her. "You are the girl who helped locate the body, aren't you?"

"How do you know about that?"

"The *Dispatch*. I didn't have your name, just your age, where you live, the fact that you're a new arrival, living with your grandmother . . . It wasn't hard to track you down by asking around. Small towns are like that."

"I don't—are—you're a reporter?" Calla asks, trying to keep up with what he's saying and with her own racing, bewildered thoughts.

"Yes, and I'm working on a story about police psychics and their role in—"

"I'm not a police psychic," Calla cuts in, casting a nervous eye at the closed door to the sunroom where her grandmother does her readings.

"No, I understand that you aren't officially working with the authorities," he's saying as Calla notices that a telltale chill is creeping into the room, "but according to the *Dispatch* piece, you—"

"I don't know what you're talking about," Calla interrupts again, shivering and looking around, "and I'm sorry, but I can't talk to you about this, so—"

"I just want to ask you a few questions about the Riggs girl and whether you think it might be connected to—"

Her grandmother's warning not to tell anyone about her role in the Riggs case ringing in her head, Calla says firmly, "I have to go. I'm sorry."

"—Monday's disappearance in Erie" is the last thing she hears in the instant before she hangs up the phone.

And there she is.

Kaitlyn.

She's standing a few feet away from Calla, looking as solid

as a living human would and wearing the same pleading expression she had the other day.

"What?" Calla asks, her heart pounding like crazy, her thoughts whirling as she wonders what the reporter was talking about while trying to grasp the fact that a dead girl has materialized in front of her yet again.

"Look, I found your b—" No, that's too harsh.

Calla takes a deep breath, pushes aside her own frustration and fear to start again. "I found you," she tells Kaitlyn as gently as she can, "in that park. Your mom has closure now. And I know how horrible this all was for you, but . . ."

I know how horrible this all was for you? her own voice echoes in disdain. *Could you be any more understated than that?*

The girl is *dead,* for God's sake. *Murdered.*

Suddenly, something else Odelia said flits into Calla's mind, bringing with it a wisp of dread.

Kaitlyn's killer is still out there somewhere.

"I'm so sorry," Calla says desperately, wearily, forcing herself to look into the girl's troubled eyes, "but I don't know how else to help you."

Kaitlyn just stares mournfully at her.

"Please . . . just tell me." *Tell me, or go away and leave me alone because you're scaring me and I'm feeling weak and strange and I don't know what to do.*

Kaitlyn is still there, but her form is beginning to seem less solid.

She's trying to stay, but she's too new at this, Calla realizes, remembering something she read in one of the books she took from Lily Dale's library. Spirits draw energy from various sources in order to materialize—sometimes from electrical sources, and sometimes from people.

"What do you want from me?" she asks again.

At last, Kaitlyn speaks. "Help her," she says cryptically.

And then, even as she begins to fade, "Stop him."

A light, warm rain is falling in Akron, Ohio, tonight. It patters on the rooftop above his rented attic bedroom and pings into the metal gutter. He barely notices the rhythmic noise as he paces. His hands are jammed into the pockets of his jeans, clenched into hard, strong fists. Angry fists.

It was all going so well.

Who would ever suspect him of an abduction and murder that took place well over a hundred miles away? And who could possibly connect him to another disappearance in Erie, Pennsylvania, more than two hours' drive in the opposite direction?

Who, indeed?

He stops pacing abruptly and snatches the *Columbus Dispatch* off his desk. It's folded open to the article that caught him completely off guard when he happened upon it earlier.

He's read it so many times since that he's memorized it by now. Memorized, in particular, the sparse details about the girl, including her age and location.

Seventeen years old. Just the right age.

Elizabeth was seventeen—and so was he—when she destroyed him.

They were supposed to go to the prom together. Blindly in love, he worked up all his courage to ask her, the most beautiful girl in the class. She said yes. She was smiling when she said it.

No. She wasn't smiling. How could he not have realized that she was laughing at him? That it was all a joke? She already had a date to the prom, Jack Bicknell, who—with his lacrosse-team pals—put her up to it.

He showed up at her house that night in a rented blue tux, and there they all were, waiting. Taunting him. Laughing at him.

Even Elizabeth.

He cried. He actually cried, in front of all of them.

That made them laugh even harder.

Even Elizabeth.

He ran away, tried to forget, tried to forgive.

Instead, the gaping wound seemed to grow. Fester.

Graduation. Summer. College—for her, at least.

Eventually, he found her there. Destroyed her in return . . . or so he believed. Until he saw the papers the next day.

Turned out it was her sleeping roommate he stabbed that night in the dorm room. She was blond and beautiful, just like Elizabeth.

Strangely, it didn't matter when he realized it was the wrong girl. Revenge was still satisfying—even more so, because no one could possibly connect him to her, or to any of the girls who came after her. But mostly because he could do it again and again, saving the real Elizabeth for last.

He has no idea where she is now. Maybe she has a career somewhere, a home, a husband, children. A life. Someday he'll find her and she'll get what she deserves. In the meantime, there are so many others to take her place.

He wonders about the seventeen-year-old girl who led the police to Kaitlyn Riggs's body. Wonders what she looks like. If she has long blond hair.

She has to have long blond hair. They all do.

Then again . . . what if she doesn't?

"Maybe that will keep you safe," he purrs softly into the empty room, imagining her, terrified, cowering, right there in front of him. "Then again . . . maybe it won't."

He'll be the one to make that decision. Who lives. Who dies. It's all up to him.

His lips curl into a smile at the heady sense of power, and the first stirring of a familiar craving begins to creep over him.

Willow York lives with her divorced mother in a small two-story gabled cottage on a narrow, tree-shaded lane a few streets over from Odelia's place. There's no shingle above the door, fueling Calla's suspicion that Willow, unlike some of the other kids here, leads a more "normal" lifestyle, like her friends back home.

When she answers the door to Calla's knock, she's wearing a white T-shirt and gray yoga pants that ride low on her slim hips, revealing a flat stomach and tanned belly button. Her long, straight dark hair is pulled back into a neat ponytail (reminding Calla again that her own overgrown bangs could use a cut), her face is scrubbed clean of makeup . . . and she's absolutely drop-dead gorgeous, Calla decides. As beautiful as Blue Slayton is. No wonder he was drawn to her.

She wonders—not for the first time—why they broke up, and if they're really over each other.

"Come on in." Willow holds the door open and steps back into the shadowy hall. "We have to be kind of quiet. My mom's taking a nap."

"*Now?* But it's so early." Some unidentifiable emotion flickers in Willow's expression, and Calla hedges uncomfortably. "I mean . . . it's kind of late. You know. For a nap."

Willow busies herself closing the door, her back to Calla. "She's doing some late readings tonight. She likes to rest up for them."

"Oh." So Willow's mother *is* a medium.

Okay, is that really any surprise?

Yes. It shouldn't be, but it is. If only because Calla still isn't used to the local industry . . . and because, okay, Willow seems so . . . normal.

Evangeline, Jacy, even Blue . . .

Well, they're all so different from anyone Calla has ever met before. Orphaned Evangeline talks freely about the spirit world and her own gifted heritage; foster-kid Jacy is so quietly, yet obviously, spiritual; Blue, whose mother left when he was little, often refers to his celebrity medium father.

Unlike the others, Willow—beautiful, smart, quiet, sophisticated—would fit in perfectly at Calla's private school back in Florida, where the other kids' parents are doctors and lawyers and bankers, like Calla's mother.

Mom.

Darrin.

Aiyana.

Kaitlyn Riggs.

The phone call from that reporter.

The chain of thoughts clicks through like falling dominoes in Calla's head. It's all she can do to come up with an answer when Willow turns around, looking relaxed again, and asks if she wants anything to drink.

"No, I'm good," she manages, and follows Willow through a small living room that's similar in size, woodwork, decor, and even clutter to her grandmother's house, and Ramona's and Paula's as well.

The rest of the first floor—dining room, kitchen, and the study—is just as ordinary, from the worn furniture to the dishes piled in the sink.

For some reason, Calla was expecting something a little more . . . upscale. Maybe not along the lines of the Slaytons' grand home on the knoll above the lake, which Calla has seen only from afar, but she just didn't picture Willow York living in a regular Lily Dale cottage that has seen better days.

In the study, a computer sits on the desk, humming in quiet activity with a simple blue-patterned screen saver that displays several icons, including, Calla notices, one for the Internet.

She casts a longing glance at it before sitting on a chair Willow offers and taking her math homework and text from her backpack.

"Thanks so much for helping me," she feels obligated to say as Willow takes a couple of sharpened pencils and a calculator from a drawer. "Not that you had any choice, but . . ."

Willow shrugs. "It's no problem. Anyway, I like math."

"Yeah, but I know there must be a million things you'd rather be doing," Calla says with a faint smile.

Willow returns it. "Maybe one or two. Come on, let's do the first problem."

Calla tries to concentrate. Really, she does. But her thoughts keep drifting back to her disturbing conversation with that reporter from the AP.

"What don't you get?" Willow asks, after showing her for the third time how to arrive at the right answer, which eludes Calla yet again.

"Pretty much everything."

Willow sighs and flips pages in the textbook. "Okay, let's backtrack a little."

Somewhere overhead, a floorboard creaks, and Calla follows Willow's upward glance.

"My mom," she says, and pushes the book toward Calla. "I'll be back in a couple of minutes. You can look over this page."

She leaves the room.

Calla waits until her footsteps have reached the second floor before darting a hand toward the computer mouse, well within arm's reach.

She clicks on the Internet icon, then swiftly types her own name and "Columbus Dispatch" into the search-engine window.

The results pop up almost instantly. Sure enough, at the top of the list is a link to an article from today's newspaper.

LOCAL GIRL LAID TO REST; GRIEVING MOM CREDITS YOUNG MEDIUM

The air is squished right out of Calla's lungs as she glances at the adjoining photo—a black-clad Elaine Riggs following a gleaming casket out of a church—and scans the article.

Footsteps overhead startle Calla, and she hears Willow call her name.

"Yeah?" Calla reaches for the mouse to click out of the screen.

"I've got to help my mom with something. I'll be a few minutes."

"Okay . . . do you mind if I check my e-mail for a second?" Calla calls impulsively.

"No, go ahead."

Perfect.

Calla quickly goes to her screen name and signs in so that she can close out the other screen when Willow returns. She really should check her e-mail . . . but not until she's read the rest of this article. Her grandmother is going to freak when she finds out about it.

She scrolls down the page and picks up reading the article where she left off.

Without warning, the screen goes dark.

Calla frowns and looks around. It's not a power outage, because the computer is still running and the lights are on.

So what hap—

Huh?

The screen is back up.

Only it no longer shows the article from the *Columbus Dispatch*.

Nor does it show Calla's e-mail.

Somehow, it's jumped to a completely different page. She must have accidentally hit something when she was scrolling down. Happens all the—

Calla's eyes widen as she realizes she's looking at a Web site.

A Web site that was created for a missing person.

More specifically . . . a missing girl.

From Erie, Pennsylvania.

A girl named Erin Shannahan.

There's a big photo of her on the Web site.

She has long blond hair and freckles that cover her face and her bare arms, and she's smiling because she doesn't know what's going to happen to her.

No. But I know what happened to her.

Calla closes her eyes, seeing the bloodied figure facedown in the woods.

SEVEN

Calla takes a few deep breaths, trying to slow her racing heart.

Then she opens her eyes and forces herself to read the text accompanying Erin's photo. She was last seen on Monday night, leaving a college party . . . wearing jeans, flip-flops, a pale pink tank top, and a silver—

"Sorry about that," a voice says nearby.

Startled, Calla looks up to see Willow sticking her head in from the kitchen.

"Did you check your e-mail?" she asks.

"I'm just finishing." With a trembling hand, Calla hurriedly manages to click the X on the top right corner of the screen, praying the Web site will go away.

It does, giving way to her e-mail again.

"Are you sure you don't want something to drink? I'm going to get a glass of pop. Want some?"

"Sure."

Anything to buy time and pull herself back together. Calla mindlessly clicks on the mailbox icon at the top of the page and scans the list of addresses.

A familiar one jumps out at her.

KZW88@cornell.edu.

Kevin.

When he first left for college at this time last year, her in-box would hold several e-mails from him every day. As the school year went on, they grew fewer and farther between, but Calla blamed that on his being busy with his classes and studying.

Then came the breakup, and finding out about Annie.

This is the first time in a while that KZW88@cornell.edu has shown up in her mailbox, and she's so shocked to see it that everything else is momentarily forgotten.

She clicks on it and holds her breath.

Hey, Calla, it was really good to see you last week. I know you've been through a lot but it seems like you're hanging in there. Crazy coincidence that we both ended up only two hundred miles away from each other in New York State, you know? It only took me a few hours to drive from Lily Dale back to Ithaca, so if you ever need anything or whatever, don't forget I'm pretty close by. Write back when you have a chance and let me know what's up, okay? xoxo Kevin

Whoa.

Out of the clear blue sky, he pops back into her life and

signs his note the way he always did—with hugs and kisses? What's that supposed to mean?

I wish I could call Lisa right this second, she finds herself thinking. Kevin's sister might be able to shed some light on what's up with him, and whether he's trying to open the door to a renewed—what, friendship? relationship?—with Calla.

She'll try Lisa later, if she has a chance.

Meanwhile, she skims the e-mail again, warning herself not to read too much into it and not to get too worked up over it, either. Still . . .

I know you've been through a lot . . .

Yeah, no kidding. She knows he's talking about losing Mom, but he dished her a good helping of trauma when he dumped her in April, too. She grabs the mouse again and scrolls the cursor over the delete button.

But for some reason, she can't make herself press it.

"Okay, here you go." Willow is back with two glasses. "It's Diet Pepsi. Is that okay?"

"Sure, thanks." Calla hurriedly moves the cursor over to the Keep As New button and clicks it there, preserving Kevin's e-mail in her box until she can figure out what to do about it.

She's got enough to worry about right now.

Including Erin Shannahan.

There isn't a doubt in her mind that the girl who disappeared from Erie on Monday is the same girl whose bloodied body Kaitlyn Riggs showed to Calla.

She wants me to know there's a connection.

She said, "Help her."

And she said . . .

Stop him.

93

She was talking about whoever murdered her and Erin.

"Are you finished?"

Willow's voice startles Calla, and she looks up to see her gesturing at the computer screen.

"What? Oh . . . yeah. Thanks for letting me check my e-mail. I can't get online at my grandmother's, and . . . well, that's really hard to get used to."

"I bet. I should check mine for a second, too, if you don't mind. Sarita is working on some graphics for the homecoming dance flyer—we have to hand it in to the committee tomorrow—and she said she'd send it to me tonight."

"Sure, no problem." Glad for another minute or two of distraction, Calla sits back and sips her pop as Willow leans over her to take the mouse.

Maybe I should go to the police, Calla thinks, rolling the cold glass back and forth between her clammy palms. *Or at least tell Gammy what's going on. She'll know what to do.*

Then again . . .

Dad is coming here tomorrow.

Odelia might decide to send Calla back to California with him if she thinks she's getting involved in the Riggs case.

And if she does that, Calla's connection to her mother's past—and to the mystery surrounding her death—will be lost.

I have to stay here, she tells herself fiercely. *At any cost.*

She thinks again of Kaitlyn Riggs and Erin Shannahan and pushes aside a fierce stab of guilt.

I don't know how to help you, she tells them silently, and shifts her gaze absently back to the computer screen.

It takes her a moment to realize she's looking at Willow's open in-box.

The subject line HOMECOMING DANCE jumps out at her.

"Sarita hasn't sent me anything yet," Willow announces, moving the mouse toward the red X that will close out the box.

Calla glances at the address on the HOMECOMING DANCE e-mail, wondering if Willow somehow missed seeing it.

But it doesn't appear to have come from Sarita after all.

The return address is blues90@aol.com.

It doesn't take a genius—or a psychic, for that matter—to figure out it belongs to Blue Slayton.

Willow clicks on the X and the screen vanishes.

Calla notices a faint smile on her lips, though, and her mind seems to be lingering someplace else as she says, "Okay, so let's get back to work on the math or we'll be here all night. I'm sure you've got other things to do."

I'm sure you do, too, Calla thinks as she turns back to her textbook. *Like e-mailing Blue back about the homecoming dance.*

Another sleepless night.

He paces across the attic floor to the small diamond-shaped window that faces the east and stares out absently at the sky, beginning to show pinkish orange sunrise streaks.

For three days now, he's been trying to forget about that newspaper article.

The one about the Riggs girl's funeral earlier this week— and the incredible means by which her body was located in Hocking Hills State Park.

But he can't seem to forget.

If anything, he's growing angrier and more frustrated with every hour that passes. He can't sleep, can't eat, can't think of anything but that girl.

He's spent too much time covering his tracks to have it all come undone because of a seventeen-year-old stranger who claims to have some kind of magical powers.

Claims? How else could she have directed the police to Kaitlyn Riggs's body?

He prowls back and forth across his attic room, not caring that the floorboards creak beneath his feet. Sometimes the second-floor tenants pound on their ceiling with the end of a broom if he paces too much, but this morning all is quiet.

Glimpsing himself in the mirror on the far wall, he feels fury stirring in his gut. A vivid purple bruise rims his right eye.

Erin Shannahan put up one hell of a fight.

In the end, she lost. They always do. He dumped her limp body in the middle of nowhere and fled, left with a shiner he's had to mask from prying eyes all week.

Black eye. Obsessive thoughts about some psychic kid.

He needs some kind of distraction.

And he might have stumbled upon just the thing.

Abruptly, he turns back to the glowing computer screen, still open to his latest find. Perhaps a little too close to home for complete comfort, but one gets tired of travel.

Hayley Gorzynski, a junior at Saint Jude's High School, right here in Akron. She'll be playing the lead role of Sandy in a local theater production of *Grease*.

The newspaper article contains a glowing quote from Jamie Corona, the show's director.

"Casting was a no brainer," Corona says. "Hayley will make a perfect Sandy, with her long blond hair and big blue eyes."

EIGHT

Friday, September 7
3:06 p.m.

Mr. Bombeck is writing yet another excruciatingly difficult problem on the board—and Calla is wishing the last bell would hurry up and ring—when it happens. Again.

She feels the presence before she spots the source. It makes itself known in the now-familiar way: a sudden chill creeps into the classroom.

She glances toward the window, left open to air the stuffy classroom on this sultry September afternoon.

The sun is still shining, and she realizes the chill isn't coming from the window. With it comes a distinct uneasiness and an eerie, tingling sensation that creeps over Calla's skin.

Her fingers tighten around her pencil and she keeps her gaze focused on Mr. Bombeck up at the front of the room.

The presence remains, grows stronger still.

Finally, no longer able to ignore it, she turns her head. Just slightly. But far enough to spot Kaitlyn Riggs, plainly visible just a few feet away, watching her.

The dead girl's ghostly eyes beg Calla to do something.

Help her. Stop him.

Stop him.

Over and over, Kaitlyn's voice fills Calla's head, her commands growing louder, more urgent.

Stop him!

Calla closes her eyes and grips, feeling sick.

Go away, she silently begs her ghostly visitor. *Don't do this to me. Not here. Not now.*

In her mind's eye—or is it?—she sees Erin Shannahan. Not the picture from the Web site, but her body, lying facedown in the woods.

This time, though, she can see more of the scene. Trees, brush, rugged terrain . . . and a trail marker bearing the letters CKT. A ring of rocks. This time she can see charred black splinters inside the circle—an abandoned campfire site?

She zeroes in on Erin herself.

Matted blond hair, freckled arms, silver watch—

Her hand . . .

It's moving, her fingers clawing at the dirt and leaves.

She's alive!

The pencil snaps in Calla's own hand and her eyes jerk open again to see one splintered piece flying through the air.

It lands on the floor across the aisle. Jacy leans over, picks it up, and looks at her. She can feel other eyes on her as everyone sitting in the vicinity looks up to see what happened.

"Is everything all right back there?" Mr. Bombeck asks from the board.

"I'm sorry, I just . . . dropped my pencil."

She reaches to take the broken piece from Jacy, who shifts his gaze to the spot where Kaitlyn Riggs materialized.

Can he see her too? Or does he sense something?

Calla turns to find that the apparition is gone.

Stop him! Stop . . . him . . .

Her voice fades to an echo in Calla's brain before it disappears altogether as the shrill ringing of the last bell shatters the room.

"All I know," Evangeline says as they make their way toward home through a gray, muggy afternoon, "is that you have got to do something about this. If this girl is alive out there somewhere, you need to help her."

"How?" Calla shifts her backpack, filled with homework for the weekend, to her other shoulder. It seems to weigh a ton, and but it's nowhere near as heavy as the new burden of figuring out what to do about Erin.

"Call the police."

"And tell them . . . ?"

"That you think she's still alive."

"And who do I say I am?"

"You can be anonymous. If we make the call from the pay phone by the café in the Dale, it doesn't come up on Caller ID."

"But I don't even know where to tell them to look. All I saw is woods, and kind of . . . rough terrain, and a trail marker . . ."

"With CKT on it," Evangeline points out. "So let's go straight to my house and Google that on the computer—if we can beat my brother to it."

Calla considers this. "I don't know . . . my grandmother was really upset that I got involved with Kaitlyn's case."

"And if you hadn't, she'd still be out there somewhere. Her body, anyway. If Erin's still alive, you can save her life. Look at it this way—you have nothing to lose. And Erin Shannahan has everything to gain."

"Do you think we should just tell my grandmother and let her deal with it?"

"Not with your dad about to blow into town. She might decide to send you back to California with him, to keep you from getting involved in stuff like this."

"I've thought about that too," Calla said. "Well, how about your aunt?"

"No way," Evangeline says firmly. "My aunt is all caught up in some date she has tonight. Something like this will really throw her off, and she really likes this guy. He sounds normal for a change—an accountant from Westfield. She really needs a nice, normal guy. Especially after having her last boyfriend dump her for a Buffalo Jills cheerleader. I told you about that, right?"

Calla nods, distracted. Normally, Ramona Taggart's disastrous love life interests her, but right now, all she cares about is Erin Shannahan.

"Okay," she tells Evangeline, picking up her pace a little as the entrance gate to Lily Dale appears around the bend—along with Mason Taggart, who's walking toward home with a couple of friends. "Let's go to your house and Google CKT."

"And then call the police?"

"Depends on what we find."

"Come on." Evangeline breaks into a jog. "We have to get there before my brother does, or he'll cause a big stink and make us wait forever."

With her father on his way to Lily Dale, Calla can't afford to wait forever. Every second counts . . . and Erin's life is hanging in the balance.

Twenty minutes later, Calla and Evangeline are at the pay phone outside the café.

"You're sure it comes up without a number?" Calla asks Evangeline as she lifts the receiver.

"I'm positive. Go on . . . dial! Do you want me to?"

"No, I'll do it." Her hand shaking like crazy, Calla begins punching out the number she scribbled on a piece of scrap paper back at the Taggarts'.

As the phone rings on the other end, Calla quickly rehearses what she and Evangeline decided she should say.

"Erin Shannahan tip line," a male voice answers on the second ring.

"I believe Erin is still alive, and that she can be found in the Allegheny Gorge, just off the Chuck Keiper Trail, near a firepit ringed by rocks."

"Good!" Evangeline hisses. "Hang up!"

"Who is this?" the voice asks in Calla's ear.

For a split second, she's absolutely frozen. Then she abruptly clamps the phone down, trembling, on the verge of tears.

Evangeline hugs her. "That was so good. You did great."

"You swear you won't tell anyone, right?"

"Are you kidding? I'll carry this to my grave, like we said."

Calla swallows hard, not wanting to think about graves.

All she wants is to put this behind her.

As she and Evangeline walk back across Cottage Row, she says a quick, silent prayer that Erin will be found in time.

Hearing car tires crunch on the gravel in the street, Calla jumps up and hurries to look out the living room window. She knows even before she lifts the lace curtain that it's not going to be her father, but she checks anyway. Just in case her intuition, or whatever she's calling it these days, is off.

Nope. A neighbor's car pulling a rented U-haul is trundling along Cottage Row, heading toward the gate.

"Is it him?" her grandmother asks from her chair across the room. She's dressed for the occasion in a pink-and-purple floral-print dress in fairly muted—for her, anyway—colors, with a lacy brown crocheted shawl draped over her shoulders.

Calla drops the curtain. "No, it's not him."

Just more summer residents leaving Lily Dale for the off-season.

The place is fast becoming a ghost town in more ways than one—definitely a good thing, with her father coming to visit. The streets are quieter every day, no longer clogged with ailing strangers seeking physical healing, or the recently bereaved longing to make contact with their dearly beloved, or troubled visitors in need of psychic counseling.

Pacing back to the couch, Calla plops down and resumes

the impatient wait for her father's arrival from the airport, all the while wondering about Erin.

Did the tip-line person take her call seriously?

Even if he did, what if she was dead wrong, and Erin is . . . well, dead?

Calla pushes the thought from her mind.

"I wish your father had let me pick him up at the airport instead of renting a car," Odelia comments.

"I know, but he said that will make things easier, since he'll have to drive back and forth to the White Inn down in Fredonia."

"He could have stayed here."

"I know." But Calla was secretly relieved when he turned down her grandmother's offer to take her bedroom for the weekend.

"It's really no trouble," she said late last night on the phone to Calla's dad, with Calla eavesdropping, of course. "I can stay right next door at the Taggarts'. They have a pull-out couch."

Of course, Jeff wouldn't hear of that. Nor would he consider sleeping on the Taggarts' pull-out couch himself, even though Ramona made the offer via Odelia.

"I'll be more comfortable in a hotel," he insisted, and it was all settled.

Calla figures that should make his visit a little easier. There's no telling what Jeff might witness if he hangs around Odelia's house 24/7. Rarely does much time go by here without some kind of spooky activity or, at the very least, someone popping up at the front door looking for a reading.

Then again, walk-ins aren't likely in the next couple of

days. When Calla got home from her mission with Evangeline earlier, she immediately noticed that the shingle above her grandmother's door—the one that reads ODELIA LAUDER, REGISTERED MEDIUM—was conspicuously missing. Hanging from its bracket was a basket filled with yellow fall chrysanthemums.

"I always take it down to be repainted at the end of the summer season," was Odelia's explanation when Calla asked her about it.

But something in her eyes told Calla that wasn't the whole truth.

She doesn't want Dad to know, Calla realized. *She knows that if he figures out what she does for a living, he won't let me stay, and I guess she wants me to.*

Calla and her grandmother seem to have silently agreed that there will be no discussion of her grandmother's—or Lily Dale's—unique spiritualist connection while Dad is here.

Sure, he's bound to figure it out when he drives through the gate, with its sign announcing that Lily Dale is the world's largest spiritualism center.

Then again, Dad can be kind of absentminded. And it's dark out. And Calla herself didn't see the gate sign when she first arrived.

Besides, the official season is over, which means there's no one manning the gatehouse and anyone can come and go. Now that the busy daily schedule is over, many cottages are boarded up, and the summer throngs have vanished, Lily Dale looks almost like any other resort community past its prime. A resort that just happens to be the birthplace of modern spiritualism.

Maybe that's how Dad will see it. Period.

All she can do is hope.

"Do you think he decided to stop off at the hotel in Fredonia first and check in?" Odelia asks.

"No. He said he was coming straight here." Calla answered the phone when he called from the Buffalo airport an hour ago, saying he had landed and was on his way to Lily Dale.

Unable to sit and wait patiently on the couch for his arrival, she gets up again and paces across the room, wondering whether they've found Erin—or her body—yet.

"You know, time always drags when you want it to race along," Odelia comments, flipping through a magazine. "And it rushes to the finish line when you want it to drag."

"Who said that?"

Odelia looks up sharply. "*I* did. Why? Have you been hearing other . . . voices?"

Calla can't help but grin. "No, I meant who said it as a quote. Like, from someone famous."

Odelia laughs—and looks a bit relieved, Calla notices as she goes back to her pacing and keeping a restless eye on the window, trying not to think about Erin.

"This Friday-night waiting game is getting to be a habit for you, isn't it?" her grandmother asks.

"Hmm?"

"Last week at this time, you were in the same boat, waiting for your friends to show up from Florida. Remember?"

Her friends. Lisa—and Kevin.

Again, Calla's thoughts flit to the e-mail he sent. It's been in the back of her mind all day, even with everything else she's had to think about.

She impulsively tried calling Lisa a little while ago, but got only her voice mail and decided not to leave a message.

How can she even begin to explain about Erin?

And even when it comes to Kevin—well, maybe she shouldn't mention the e-mail to Lisa at all. Maybe it means only that Kevin's still sympathetic about her loss and just wanted to check in. Maybe he thinks enough time has passed since their breakup that they can just be casual friends.

Yeah, right.

Sun-streaked; tanned; wearing flip-flops, puka shells, and board shorts, he was a welcome, familiar sight. But seeing him even just for a few minutes reminded Calla that she's not quite over him yet.

Come on . . . Not quite?

Okay, not by a long shot.

Not even after spending more time with Jacy, and all the attention from Blue Slayton, and the fact that he might be asking her to the homecoming—

That thought is interrupted by the distant sound of a car approaching.

"That's my dad!" she announces to Odelia, who nods, courtesy of her own "intuition."

By the time her grandmother gets to her feet, Calla has reached the front door and is about to open it. She looks back at the last minute, worried. "Gammy," she says, "you're not going to say anything to my dad about . . . anything. Are you?"

"Are you kidding?" Odelia settles her shawl around her shoulders demurely and pulls her glasses down from her forehead to rest on the tip of her nose. She looks almost like a regular grandmother. Kind of. If you ignore her red hair and pink clogs.

Calla smiles faintly. "I didn't think you'd tell him," she says, "but I wanted to make sure. I mean, I don't want you to lie. Just . . ."

"Omit."

"Right."

"Got it."

Calla opens the door, and her breath promptly catches in her throat. There he is, climbing out of a compact rental car parked at the curb.

"Dad!" She races outside, bounds down the steps, and hurtles herself into his arms like a little girl.

Her father holds her in a fierce bear hug and it feels so good, so incredibly good, that she almost cries.

Okay, maybe she is crying a little. Embarrassed, she ducks her head when he releases her and wipes her eyes before looking up at him.

"How was your trip?" she asks, noticing that there are a few light strands in his black hair just above his ears and for a split second she thinks they must be blond, bleached from the California sun. Then she realizes they're gray. Gray hair. Dad's face looks different, too. He's not wearing his glasses—maybe that's why. He wore them a lot after Mom died. All those tears kept interfering with his contact lenses. But he's got them on again today, so maybe that's a sign that he's not crying as much.

His familiar black eyes might not be bloodshot and red rimmed anymore, but they're not twinkling at Calla the way they used to, either.

"My trip was a breeze," Dad says, and she can tell he's trying to sound upbeat. "Everything went right on time, no problem making the connection in New York . . . it makes me feel like you're just a hop, skip, and a jump away from me, instead of a whole continent."

She sees him turn his head, looking at something over her shoulder, and follows his gaze to see her grandmother standing on the porch. It's not like her to hold back, but she seems to be keeping her distance, giving them some space.

She gives a little wave.

Jeff waves back.

Then Odelia comes slowly down the steps, and they share a slightly awkward-looking hug.

"It's good to see you, Jeff," Odelia says with affection. "How have you been?"

"Hanging in there," he replies as a door slams next door.

Calla spots Ramona stepping out onto the Taggarts' porch, bathed in a yellow glow from the overhead light fixture.

"Hi, everyone," she calls cheerfully, breezing down the front steps with her car keys in hand.

"Ramona, hi . . . come meet Calla's dad," Odelia invites.

Uh-oh. Not such a good idea. But Calla does a quick scan and is glad to see that the shingle above Ramona's door is cast in shadows from low-hanging boughs. Dad can't possibly read it from way over here.

"That's my friend Evangeline's aunt," Calla tells her father as Ramona comes toward them, jangling not just from the keys she's carrying but from the jewelry she's wearing. Calla decides she looks like a pretty gypsy, with her hoop earrings, stacked bracelets, long gauzy skirt, and brown ringlets that fall past her shoulders.

"Hi—Jeff, right?" Ramona says easily, arriving in front of them and holding out her hand. "I'm Ramona Taggart."

"Nice to meet you."

As Calla watches her father shake Ramona's hand, a crazy vision flashes through her brain. So crazy she decides she must be losing it. Seriously.

There is absolutely no way on earth her father and Ramona Taggart could ever possibly have any kind of . . .

Connection.

Romantic, or anything else.

Ramona is a total free spirit, as much a gypsy on the inside as she appears to be on the outside. She's the exact opposite of Mom, a level-headed, conservative, ultraorganized business-woman.

Anyway, Dad was crazy about Mom. Now that she's gone, Calla can't imagine him with anyone else.

Especially Ramona, of all people.

So much for my "intuition."

"I hope Odelia told you that you're welcome to stay at our place," Ramona is saying.

"Thanks, I mean, she did mention it—and that's really nice of you—but I couldn't do that." Dad looks flustered.

I don't even know you. That, Calla realizes, is what he's think-ing. He doesn't yet understand that the people here in western New York are pretty much the friendliest, most welcoming people Calla has ever met anywhere, including down South.

"Are you sure?" Ramona asks. "I've got plenty of room."

"I've already got a hotel room booked. But . . . thanks again."

"Well, if you change your mind . . . I'll be home late, but the front door's open. Literally."

"Hot date?" Odelia calls after her, and Ramona just laughs and heads toward her car.

Again, Calla wonders if there might be a glimmer of something between Dad and—

No. No way. Impossible.

"Brrr . . . it's chilly out here," Odelia comments. "Come on, let's go inside."

"Okay," Dad agrees, "but I just want to grab my contact lens solution and my glasses out of my bag in the trunk. My eyes are burning from all that dry air on the plane."

"Go ahead. I'll get dinner on the table. I made fried chicken."

"That's my favorite," Dad says. "I haven't had it in years."

Calla meets her grandmother's gaze and knows that she, too, is thinking of her mother.

Suddenly, she longs to tell her father that fried chicken was once Mom's favorite, too. That, and all the other things she's learned about her mother since arriving in Lily Dale. But she can't just start blurting information. She has to wait until the time is right.

Odelia disappears into the house, leaving the two of them alone together on the shadowy street. Calla tries to think of something to say. Something casual and conversational.

Funny, she still isn't used to having a one-on-one relationship with her father. They were always a family of three. Dad was there, but Calla talked more to her mother—even if she's more like her father in temperament and attitude.

Standing beside her father as he rummages through his small duffel, she thinks of her mother's frequent business trips and the fancy rolling luggage she always packed full of her sophisticated clothing. Mom and Dad really were different in so many ways.

Ramona toots the horn as she drives past on her way toward the gate.

"She seems nice." Dad tucks a small leather pouch under his arm and closes the trunk.

"Yeah. She's great. She knew Mom," Calla tells him, and seeing the troubled look on her father's face, is instantly sorry.

"Back in high school, they were friends, sort of. Mom was older and Ramona used to look up to her, and she's been telling me what Mom was like back then," Calla says in a rush, trying to smooth things over and realizing she's only making it worse, judging by Dad's expression.

"Your mother never liked to talk about her past. She didn't look back. She wasn't that kind of person."

"I know. That's why I like being here. It makes me feel closer to her—well, to a *her* I never knew until now."

And maybe I don't even know the Mom we both lived with for all these years.

Again, she thinks of the Saint Patrick's Day visit from Darrin.

Mom had secrets. Does Dad realize that? Would it hurt him now to know about the visit from her old boyfriend?

Does it even matter if it hurts him, if her death was no accident and Darrin's visit might be linked to it?

Maybe Dad does know about that, anyway, Calla reminds

herself. *Maybe Dad has secrets too, even. Maybe you're the only one who's been in the dark all these years.*

Mom was so sympathetic back in April when Kevin broke up with Calla, though. Wouldn't she have mentioned her own high school romance, especially if she'd seen her ex-boyfriend just weeks earlier?

She might have . . . if the recent visit were innocent. Two old friends catching up on old times.

Come on, Calla! Darrin was using a fake name. How is that innocent in any possible way?

As Ramona had told her, he supposedly vanished from Lily Dale without a trace twenty years ago. Why? What did that have to do with Mom? Or with Mom's death?

Calla wishes desperately that she'd had the chance to talk to Jacy about all of this. Now it's going to have to wait until after Dad leaves. And while he's here, she'd better not say anything more.

"Ready to go inside?" she asks her father.

"Sure." He puts an arm around her shoulders as they walk together up the steps of Mom's childhood home.

What on earth would he do without the Internet?

It's made everything so much easier.

He can use it to keep track of the police proceedings that surround Kaitlyn Riggs's murder and Erin Shannahan's disappearance, making sure they're not coming too close for comfort.

He can scour newspapers online for photos of local high school girls—girls like Hayley Gorzynski, with long blond hair—whose pretty faces beam at the camera. They're so proud to have landed on the varsity team or in the honor society or whatever it is that brought a photographer to their school. Does it ever occur to them that someone like him might be watching them? Don't they realize how easy it is for him to find out where they live? To follow them as they go about their daily routines until the time is right to strike?

The Internet is good, too, for atlas information.

Now, sitting in front of his desktop computer in his attic apartment, he clicks the mouse to zero in on the map.

Lily Dale, New York—that's not far from Erie. Maybe another half hour's drive northeast past the Pennsylvania border, an easy trip up the New York State Thruway. He already checked the mileage. The population, too.

He might not have that girl psychic's name, but Lily Dale is a small town. And small-town people can be surprisingly trusting. Sometimes they don't even lock their doors.

Never a good idea, he chides mockingly.

Small-town folks are usually friendly, too.

Even to strangers asking questions—say, about young female newcomers who live with their grandmothers.

"This was fun, tonight." Calla's father sounds almost surprised as she walks him to the front door.

"It was, wasn't it?" She smiles, thinking the evening went much better than she could have hoped.

She and her father and grandmother ate fried chicken and talked easily about food, Odelia's cooking, Calla's new school, her father's new job. Calla kept bracing herself for sticky topics—about her mother and Lily Dale—to pop up, but they never did.

Odelia went up to bed a half hour ago, leaving them to catch up until Dad caught Calla yawning and decided it was time to go.

"Get some sleep," he tells her now as she opens the door for him.

"You, too."

"I'll try. It's barely eight o'clock in California. It figures—now that I've finally set my body clock to the West Coast time zone, here I am back in the East. I'll probably be up until the middle of the night."

"Well, don't oversleep. Gammy wants you here early for her special breakfast, remember?"

"Who could forget homemade blueberry waffles with whipped cream?" Dad kisses her on the cheek. "Okay, see you in the morning, Cal. Sweet dreams."

Yeah—I can only hope.

As she watches him drive away, Calla remembers all those nights she woke at 3:17 after the recurring nightmare about Mom, Odelia, and dredging the lake. That hasn't happened lately—not since she figured out the Saint Patrick's Day connection.

And stalled right there.

Again, she wonders what happened between her mother and Darrin, and what that has to do with Mom's death.

That thought process leads naturally to Erin. Calla was so busy all night, she didn't have much time to dwell on it.

Now, though, she goes straight for the television remote. Odelia's cable brings in a local television station from Erie, and the eleven o'clock news should be starting in a few minutes.

There's going to be news about Erin, she tells herself as she settles on the couch. *I just know it.*

She's right. It's the top story.

"A happy ending tonight to a story we've been following all week," the anchor announces over footage of a rural area swarming with people, police cars, rescue vehicles, and satellite trucks. "Seventeen-year-old Erin Shannahan, missing since Labor Day, was found alive just hours ago in the Allegheny Gorge."

Calla gasps, clasping her hands to her mouth.

"Acting on an anonymous tip, police searched the rugged Chuck Keiper Trail, where the girl was ultimately spotted by a helicopter. She was transferred via ambulance to an unnamed local hospital, where she is listed in critical condition but is expected to survive."

Expected to survive. Thank God, thank God.

"Relatively warm overnight temperatures this week are credited with helping to keep her alive. With a cold front headed in late tomorrow, the window of opportunity for rescue was rapidly drawing to a close. Police are releasing no further details about the girl's disappearance, or about the tip that led them to her, and the case remains under active investigation. In other news . . ."

Calla tosses the remote aside and hurries to the front door. She opens it and looks out at the Taggarts' driveway, noting that the lights are on, and Ramona's car is still gone. Good.

She slips out into the night and across the yard. She's halfway up the steps when the front door opens and Evangeline appears, wearing a pair of lavender knit pajamas and sneakers.

"Oh! Calla! You scared me!"

"Evangeline, did you see—"

"Yes! I just saw it. I was about to run over to your house and cross my fingers you were still up. I can't believe it!"

"I can't, either!"

Their excited whispers punctuate the hushed night air, marked only by steadily chirping crickets and the occasional croak of a frog.

"You must feel great," Evangeline tells her. "You just saved a life. I told you calling the hotline was the right move."

Wrong move, he silently snarls at the so-called anonymous tipster as he strides angrily across the floor like a caged animal.

He should have been more careful. Made sure Erin Shannahan was dead before he dumped her. Now she's going to tell the cops all about the so-called detective who abducted her.

That simply can't happen.

He'll take care of Erin Shannahan once and for all.

But first, he has to silence little Miss Psychic. There isn't a doubt in his mind that she's the one who led the police to Erin. Thanks to his online research, he already knows exactly how far away she is, and exactly where to find her, if the time comes.

No . . .

Not if.

When the time comes.

You might have saved one life—temporarily, he tells her, *but you just made sure you're going to lose your own.*

NINE

Saturday, September 8
10:45 a.m.

"More coffee, Jeff?"

"Sure, I'll take a warm-up. Thanks."

Stifling a yawn, Calla watches her grandmother fill her father's cup. He sits comfortably at the kitchen table eating breakfast as though they've all done this a thousand times before.

"Tired, Cal?" he asks, catching her yawn.

"I stayed up awhile after you left."

Awhile? More like hours. Too exhilarated to sleep after the news about Erin, she watched a couple of bad old movies on television. Today, she's paying the price with burning shoulder blades and scratchy eyelids—just like all those mornings when she was awakened at 3:17 and couldn't get back to sleep.

"That was delicious, Odelia." Dad polishes off his second

helping of homemade waffles with fresh blueberries and whipped cream. "I think I've got to go walk this off. How about showing me around Lily Dale, Cal?"

"Oh, uh, there's not much to see, really."

Conscious of her grandmother looking up, mid-sip, above the rim of her coffee cup, she goes on nervously, "I mean, it's a small town." *Which happens to be populated by mediums, channelers, healers, and a whole lot of dead people.* "You know . . . just a bunch of houses . . ." *Yeah, mostly haunted.* ". . . And, uh, you know, some trees."

Uh-huh. Including one former tree: the concrete-encased Inspiration Stump deep in Leolyn Woods—a hallowed local landmark where the Dale's spiritual energy is supposedly at its peak.

"I don't care what we see," Dad tells her, "as long as we can get out and enjoy a beautiful day." He gestures at the sun streaming in the window, and Calla curses it for making one of its rare local appearances today, of all days.

"But I was thinking we could go to a movie or something," she suggests. "I've been wanting to see . . . uh . . . uh . . ." Terrific—she can't come up with one title of a movie that might be playing right now.

That's what happens when you're completely out of touch with the electronic world. The only movie that pops into her head is a really old, really stupid comedy from the early eighties that was on late last night.

It's one she watched with Kevin on a rainy night when he was home last winter break. She still remembers everything about that night—the way they cuddled on the couch in their sweats, eating hot brownies she had baked for them; the way they laughed, not at the lame movie, but at themselves for watching it; the way Kevin looked and smelled and tasted, like molten chocolate, when he kissed her.

She pushes the memory away, telling her father, "I've, uh, been wanting to see . . . something funny. A good comedy. There are a bunch of them out now." Total guess, of course.

Maybe a good one because her father says, "I know, and I could use a good laugh, too."

"Great. So let's go to the movies. Want to come, Gammy?"

"Can't right now . . . I've got a meeting."

Right—for the mediums' league. Which, of course, she doesn't mention.

"It's okay, we'll go to the movies tonight instead," Dad says. "For right now, I'd love to get outside since there's no smog for a change."

"Smog? In Lily Dale?" Odelia smiles.

"Have I told you how bad the smog is where I am?" Dad asks, and shakes his head.

"I thought you liked California, Dad."

"I do. Except for the smog. Anyway, the leaves are starting to turn here. We have to get outside. I haven't seen fall foliage in years."

Calla hasn't seen it *ever*.

She glances toward the window above the sink and notices, for the first time, a few golden and reddish leaves among the branches. She's been so preoccupied, she hasn't even noticed them until now. Or maybe they weren't there until now?

Whatever, the bright foliage is a blatant reminder that the season is turning at last. Summer, which brought Mom's tragic death, is almost behind them now.

Back in Florida—and out in California, come to think of it—seasons don't come and go with much visible change. There's always sun and green foliage, blooming flowers, and blue skies. No obvious seasonal closure. Not like here.

So. Maybe the changing landscape will help bring some kind of closure to the raw wound.

Yet another reason why it's good that Calla's here in Lily Dale . . . and why it's a good idea for her to stay awhile.

Dad pushes back his chair and picks up his plate, carrying it to the sink.

"Leave it, Jeff. I'll get the dishes," Odelia says promptly. "Really. It takes two seconds to wash them."

"Then I'll dry and Calla can put away."

"Oh, we don't dry or put away," Odelia says. "That's a waste of time. Around here, we pretty much just leave them in the dish rack to dry by themselves. Right, Calla?"

"She does," Calla tells her father. "She says why bother to put stuff away when you're just going to use it all again later?"

Dad grins and shakes his head.

Less than five minutes later, Calla finds herself walking down sun-splashed Cottage Row with him. Sure enough, the boughs overhead seem to have changed overnight, with lots of yellows and golds tucked among the green leaves, and even a few shades of red.

The sun is bright but not particularly warm today; the air is crisp with a breeze off the lake.

She thinks about Erin. About how she might not have survived another night—a cold night—in the woods.

How did she get there? Was the person who hurt her also responsible for Kaitlyn's death?

Yes. There isn't a doubt in Calla's mind about that, after the way Kaitlyn urgently told her to "Stop him."

But did she?

I found Erin, she thinks uneasily. *I helped her, like Kaitlyn asked.*

But did I stop him?

I don't even know who he is. What if the police don't find him?

"Huh."

Startled by Dad's voice, she looks up to see that they've made it halfway down the block, and he's gazing at a nearby cottage.

More like, at the shingle hanging from a porch post on the cottage.

PATSY METCALF, REGISTERED MEDIUM & SPIRITUAL CONSULTANT

"I feel like I'm in California all over again," Dad comments with a laugh.

Uh-oh. To distract him, Calla points at the patch of water visible between the houses and trees. "Look, Dad . . . isn't it pretty?"

"Beautiful."

"Let's head down that way. There's a nice little dock and benches by the water." And it's away from all the houses—and signs.

As they head closer to the lake, Calla can see that today, for a change, it actually looks more blue than gray. She can hear the distant hum of a fishing boat.

"Have you been swimming a lot here, Cal?"

"Not at all."

"Why not? You always love the water."

"Yeah, but it's too cold for me here," she says, not about to tell him the real reason she hasn't gone in.

"It's pretty cold in California, too . . . the Pacific, I mean."

"Have you been in it?" she asks in surprise. Her father never went to the beach back in Florida. Mom, either. That wasn't their thing.

Calla often went out to Pass-a-Grille Beach with Lisa, though. And later, with Kevin. She shoves aside the memory of him, tanned and bare chested in board shorts, diving into the warm, salty Gulf of Mexico surf with his boogie board.

"I've gone up to Malibu once or twice," her father tells her. "Dan surfs, so he goes up all the time." Dan is the friend Dad's staying with out there. "He talked me into it."

"Did you try surfing?" She's wide-eyed at the thought of her father in a bathing suit, let alone on a surfboard.

"Yeah . . . tried and failed." He laughs. "But it was actually fun. I might try it again."

Wow. Maybe she doesn't know him as well as she thought she did.

That's a strange feeling. Just as it was when she figured out that there might have been more to her mother than Calla ever knew when she was alive.

Is this what it's like when you grow up and drift apart from your family? Do you start seeing your parents less as *parents,* more as just . . . *people?*

People with quirks and faults and secrets.

A fresh sense of loss sweeps through Calla. It isn't fair. She'll never have the chance to be an adult alongside her mother—to be women together. She was cheated out of that.

Nobody ever said life was supposed to be fair.

Anyway, Dad's going to be around. And she's going to grow up, and they're going to have to build some kind of relationship, some kind of life. In California or Florida or . . . wherever. Just the two of them.

They walk along and Calla kicks a pebble a few times, thinking the silence is awkward. She has to say something, anything, to break it.

"So, Dad . . . does Lily Dale look like you pictured it?"

"I never really tried to picture it, I don't think. Not until you came to stay here, anyway."

"Really?"

He shakes his head. "All I knew was that it was a small town by a lake, with long, stormy winters. And that Mom left when she graduated from high school."

"And never looked back," Calla murmurs. "Right?"

"Right. Calla . . ." Dad pauses as though he's weighing his words carefully before going on. "Your mother didn't have the happiest childhood here. Her father left when she was young, and your grandmother . . . well, I'm sure she did her best, but she's not the most stable person I've ever known."

"I know, but she's—"

"Look, Odelia's been great through all of this. To you and to me, too, even. That's why this feels so . . . strange."

"What does?"

"Being here." He looks around, waves a hand at the row of cottages, and at the lake visible beyond. "Because I never got the feeling your mother had any intention of coming back. Even to visit."

"Did she say that?"

"No. We didn't talk about it."

"Ever?"

He shrugs. "She didn't want to and I didn't push her. So even though I can understand your wanting to know more about her life here, I don't think it's something she carried with her after she left."

Calla could tell him that he might be wrong about that, but that would only open the door to something neither of them is prepared to handle right now.

Dad clears his throat, but his voice still sounds ragged when he goes on. "I think Mom would just want you to remember her how—and where—she was when she was a part of your life. *Our* lives."

Calla's eyes fill with tears, and she looks down, trying hard not to cry.

"Cal, I'm sorry." Dad stops walking and puts a gentle hand on her arm.

"For what?" She wipes her eyes on the sleeve of her sweatshirt and looks up. He's blurry. She is crying, dammit.

"For upsetting you about Mom. I know it's hard for you. It's hard for me, too. Look, maybe . . . maybe when I go back to California, you should come with me. Forget about staying here another month or two and just—"

"No!" she cuts in. "I can't do that, Dad! I mean, where would I even stay?"

"I'm sure we could work something out with Dan and—"

"But I can't!" she says again, trying not to sound frantic. "I mean, I've got my babysitting job here now, and Paula's counting on me, and anyway . . . I shouldn't leave when I'm having all this trouble in math," she adds without thinking, grasping at straws.

126

"What trouble in math?" he asks sharply.

Oops. She wasn't going to tell him about that.

She quickly explains the situation, trying to make the issue sound important enough that she should stay here and get caught up on the curriculum, but not so urgent that her father will be concerned about her academics and pull her out of Lily Dale High.

"I'm already getting back on the right track," she assures him, "so you don't have to worry."

"Too late. I'm worried. You're about to start applying to colleges. You need to keep your grades up."

College? That's the last thing on her mind with all that's gone on.

Back before Mom died, they used to talk about where she would apply, and the trips they would take together to visit various campuses. Mom—who put herself through a state university, then got an Ivy League MBA—wanted Calla to get into a good school. When Kevin was accepted into Cornell, Mom was probably even more thrilled than Mrs. Wilson was.

Calla used to think, somewhere in the back of her mind, that she might follow him there someday. Not because of any burning academic ambition, though. More because she was crazy about Kevin and wanted to be near him.

Well, that's clearly not an option now. She doesn't know what she wants to do next year.

And there's not a whole lot of time to figure it out.

"Dad, I've got a great study partner for math," she says, "and the teacher is on top of it, too. And anyway, you know it wouldn't be good for me to start yet another new school right away. That won't look great on my college applications either."

"You're right." He flashes a sad smile. "I guess I just wish I hadn't agreed to this plan in the first place."

"It was a good plan. And I'm in good hands here between school and Gammy."

"I know. I just wish they were my hands. And Mom's."

She swallows hard, aching, closing her eyes.

After a moment, she feels his arms settling around her shoulders, holding her close. The hug is so comforting that she just sinks into it, glad he's here.

Then she hears him speak and is startled to realize his voice isn't as close by as it should be.

The arms release her just as she opens her eyes to see that her father is still a few feet away, and his hands are shoved into the pockets of his khakis.

TEN

"What . . . what did you say, Dad?" Calla asks, shaken, looking around, seeing no one.

Someone hugged her. Someone invisible. Because it couldn't have been her father.

"I said, I'm selfish. I miss you."

Calla nods vaguely, unable to speak, sensing the presence just beside her. A comforting presence. Not like Kaitlyn's. Or even Aiyana's.

Mom? Is that you?

She reaches out, half expecting to encounter something—someone—solid and finding only thin air.

Are you here? Oh, Mom . . . I need you so much.

Oblivious, her father sighs. "Listen, Cal, if you came back to California with me now, we could make it work."

That jars her enough to find her voice, and she manages to say, "I really want to stay awhile longer. Like we said. Please?"

"I'll think about it," he says, and the subject is dropped.

Or so it seems.

They walk a few more steps, and her father suddenly says, "That's bizarre."

Calla looks up to see him frowning at the shingle on the next house down.

REV. DORIS HENDERSON, CLAIRVOYANT.

Here we go, she thinks, the lingering warmth of the phantom hug evaporating.

"What's bizarre?" she asks her father, and holds her breath, waiting for a reply.

"Two New Age freaks living right next to each other in the middle of nowhere."

She should have known the local trade couldn't stay hidden for very long.

"New Age freaks? Geez, Dad." She's so irritated at his phrasing that she forgets, for a moment, about trying to distract him.

Then, remembering that her future here could very well be hanging in the balance, she looks around and points at a bird flying overhead. "Hey, wow, is that a bald eagle? Look! They're not on the endangered list anymore, you know."

Her father glances up. "That's a sparrow."

Then he says, reading off a shingle on the next house down, "*Andy Brighton, Psychic Medium,*" and Calla realizes it's all over.

"Andy's a friend of Gammy's, Dad."

"Really." His tone says, *that just figures.*

"Yeah, and his cat just had kittens and we're getting one— I mean, she's getting one—in a few days. Isn't that cool? I've always wanted a pet."

"Mmm-hmm. So he's a medium? What does that mean, exactly?"

"Oh, you know."

"No," her father says evenly, "I don't."

"He . . . helps people."

"By doing what?"

"I don't know." That's sort of the truth. "I mean, I've never seen him do it."

Her father looks around, rubbing his chin.

Then he says, slowly, "Is it just me, or are an awful lot of people around here . . ."

"New Age freaks?" she can't help but say when he trails off. She's feeling prickly—and defensive—so she clamps her mouth shut before she really shoves her foot in and ruins everything.

"You said it, not me," he tells her with a shrug, then admits, "this time, anyway." He smiles faintly to show her he didn't mean anything by it.

Deciding to forgive him, Calla says, "Yeah, there are a few mediums around here." *Okay, dozens, but who's counting?*

"That's interesting."

He really does seem intrigued. So much so that Calla suddenly decides to take the opposite tack, thinking maybe it's better to enlighten than obscure the facts.

"Well, over a hundred years ago, Lily Dale was actually the birthplace of the spiritualist religion, you know, so . . ."

"So these mediums have been hanging around here for, what, a hundred years?" he asks with a grin.

She can't help but smile back. "I guess so."

"What do they do? Have seances and read crystal balls?"

Calla can't help but notice that he sounds pretty igno-rant . . . and exactly like she did on her first day here.

Again, she realizes how far she's come in such a short time. How Lily Dale's extraordinariness now feels incredibly ordinary.

To her father, aloud, she says only, "I haven't had readings with any of them, so I don't really know what they do."

Which is the truth.

And he seems satisfied, because he changes the subject to what kind of fish are found in Cassadaga Lake.

"I don't know how long it's been since I last went to a movie," Odelia comments from the front seat beside Calla's father as he drives along Cottage Row late Saturday night. "That was so good. Thanks for asking me to join you two, Jeff."

"You're welcome. And maybe next time, I won't have to practically drag you along."

"Well, you know, it's past my bedtime."

Yeah, right. In the backseat, Calla smiles. She knows why her grandmother was so resistant to the invitation—she wanted Calla and her father to spend time alone together.

But that's the last thing Calla wanted tonight. By the end of the day spent walking around Lily Dale, eating lunch and doing some shopping together down in Dunkirk, she had run out of things to say to her father. He did think to ask if she needed any clothes when they passed a T.J. Maxx store, and she admitted she could use a couple of sweaters and a warm coat.

But shopping with her father isn't the same as shopping with her mother. Mom used to come into the dressing room with her and check out everything she tried on. Dad milled around looking bored while trying to be patient.

In the end, Calla chose only one sweater and an inexpensive down coat, feeling guilty about making him spend any money on her though he kept asking if she was sure that was all she needed. She couldn't bring herself to tell him she desperately needs more clothes and a haircut. Not that she thinks he's so broke he can't afford a haircut, but she dreads the thought of dragging him to a salon on the heels of shopping.

She still isn't used to being a twosome with him. It's not that it's awkward, necessarily. More just . . . depressing. And a little tense, at times.

Maybe Dad feels the same way, because he was pretty insistent about bringing Odelia along tonight.

First they saw a hilarious movie, then they went to dinner at Rocco's, a cozy, crowded Italian restaurant in nearby Fredonia. The conversation flowed easily over calamari and fettucine. Odelia had them laughing as she told stories of her daily adventures—somehow managing to leave out any hint of what she does for a living. She was great company, as always.

There's another reason Calla wanted Gammy with them tonight: so Dad would see how comfortable she is with her grandmother. Plus, she figured she'd have an ally this time if they got into another debate.

Not that the subject of her returning to California with him has come up at all since this morning. Still, it's there, still simmering just under the surface, waiting to be resolved.

"Oh, look, there are the Taggarts," Odelia comments as Jeff pulls up in front of her cottage.

Calla sees the flickering glow of a lit candle from the porch next door.

Like most people around here, Calla's noticed, Evangeline's family likes to be outdoors whenever possible. At night, in the rain, whatever. Maybe it's because the weather in Lily Dale is so harsh for much of the year, summer and early fall are the only times they can take advantage of fresh air.

In Florida, it's the polar opposite—that's the time of year when people spend more time indoors, thanks to harsh weather in the form of heat, humidity, and ominous thunderstorms, not to mention hurricane season.

"Dad, you have to come meet Evangeline," Calla tells him, thinking that might make him more willing to see the advantages of her staying in Lily Dale. Here, at least, she has a friend.

She expects an argument from him—he just mentioned how tired he is despite the time change from California, and that he's looking forward to crawling into bed back at the White Inn.

But he says, "All right," and promptly turns off the car engine, and Calla has another illogical flash about him and Ramona. Which she immediately pushes right back out of her head.

The beautiful day turned into a beautiful night: a fat white moon perched in an unusually cloudless black sky glittering with stars. Night insects chirp a steady rhythm, and somewhere in the distance, a dog is barking nonstop. It's chilly, and Calla is glad she's wearing her new sweater.

"How was the movie?" Ramona calls as the three of them walk toward her porch, where she and Evangeline are lounging on wicker furniture, illuminated only by candlelight from a mesh-covered green glass globe.

"How did you know we went to a movie?" Calla asks, and instantly regrets it. Maybe Ramona knew the way other people around here know things—and will say it in front of Dad.

"Odelia told me," is the reply, to Calla's relief.

Calla glances up, reassured to find that the resident shingle—RAMONA TAGGART, REGISTERED MEDIUM—is safely shrouded in shadow.

"What'd you see?" Evangeline asks.

"The new one with Steve Carell. I love him," Calla tells her. "Hey, this is my dad. Dad, Evangeline. And you already met Ramona."

"It's nice to meet you, Mr. Delaney," Evangeline says politely, reaching down over the railing to shake Dad's hand—and automatically scoring some points, Calla sees.

"Come on up and sit with us for a little bit," Ramona invites. "It's supposed to be freezing out by morning, and we can't stand the thought of going inside yet."

Calla looks at her father, anticipating a "thanks, but no thanks." Instead, he shrugs, saying, "Maybe for a few minutes."

"I'm so sorry for your loss," Ramona tells him as they climb the steps. "I should have said that last night, first thing."

"Oh . . . thank you," Dad says politely.

There's an awkward moment of silence until Odelia pipes up, "How was your date, Ramona? I forgot to ask you earlier."

"He was a jerk."

"Oh, no . . . again?"

Calla really hopes they won't get into detail. Ramona told her grandmother the other day that lately every man she dates runs screaming from her the moment he finds out what she does for a living.

"Aren't they all?" Ramona asks with a shrug, twirling the stem of her wineglass back and forth in her palms. She's barefoot, wearing old jeans with tattered hems. In this light, her face looks really pretty. Calla finds herself wondering if Dad is noticing.

"Someday you'll find someone worthy of you, hon," Odelia tells her.

"I'm not holding my breath for that. So . . . have a seat. Can I get you a glass of wine, Jeff? Odelia? Calla, some pop?"

"Pop!" Dad blurts out, and they all look at him.

"Oh, sorry." He grins. "That just caught me off guard. That's what we always called it back when I was growing up—I'm from Chicago. And it's what Stephanie used to call it, too . . . back when we first met."

Ramona laughs. "Must be a Midwestern thing."

"This isn't the Midwest," Evangeline protests.

"Sometimes it feels that way, though," her aunt tells her. "So . . . Jeff . . . wine? Pop?"

"Nothing for me."

Odelia wants a glass of wine, though, and Calla agrees to a Pepsi.

"I'll get it," Evangeline tells her aunt, and shoots Calla a look.

"I'll come with you," Calla decides promptly. They haven't had a chance to catch up since they found out about Erin last night.

"While you're at it"—legs draped over the arm of her chair, Ramona dangles her bare toes in the air—"tell your brother his time is up on the computer."

"It was up a half hour ago."

"I know." Ramona sighs. "I swear, Mason would be online

twenty-four-seven if I allowed it. Between these two kids, do I ever even get a chance to use my own computer? No."

Feeling guilty about her own intrusion on Ramona's computer time, Calla follows Evangeline inside.

"How's it going?" Evangeline immediately asks in a whisper.

"So far, so good. He hasn't figured out anything yet. Make sure you don't slip."

"I won't. And my aunt won't, either. She knows the deal. Did you hear anything else about Erin?"

"No, but I've been out of touch all day. Have you?"

"I checked online earlier and there was some stuff about her being found."

"Did they catch the guy who did it yet?" Calla asks breathlessly, and feels a stab of fear when Evangeline shakes her head.

"They hadn't when I last looked, anyway," she adds, "but maybe something's happened by now. Come on, let's go kick Mason off the computer so we can check."

They cross the living and dining rooms with their comfortable household disorder and head into the den, where they find Mason.

He shares his sister's slightly frizzy reddish hair, round face, and hazel eyes, only his are more solemn, deeply set behind owlish glasses.

"You have to get off the computer," Evangeline announces.

"In a few minutes." Mason is fixated on the screen, not even bothering to look at them. He's caught up in a game of RuneScape, as usual.

"No, now. Aunt Ramona said."

"In a few minutes."

"Now," Evangeline insists with big-sister authority. "Calla needs to use it." Evangeline might as well add a sassy *So there*.

Mason looks at Calla. "You need the computer?"

She hedges. "Not right this second."

"But you *can* use it right this second," Evangeline tells Calla, "because he's getting off right this second. Like Aunt Ramona said."

Mason scowls, clicks the mouse, and shoves back his chair. "Whatever," he grumbles, and leaves the room.

Evangeline grins at Calla. "Sometimes I love being the oldest."

"And sometimes I'm totally glad I'm an only child."

"Really?"

"Okay, not really." Actually, it's not something she ever thought much about until lately.

If she had a sister or brother, she wouldn't feel quite so alone since her mother's death.

For a moment, she imagines what it would be like to have a sister and is caught off guard by an almost overwhelming sense of longing. The ache is so acute that it's almost a loss . . . almost as though she's mourning not just her mother but a person who never even existed.

My sister.

Seeing movement out of the corner of her eye, Calla turns her head and there, standing beside her, is Aiyana.

ELEVEN

Aiyana's solemn expression is almost . . . knowing.

As if she's telling Calla she can read her thoughts, and . . .

And what? What's going on?

"So should we check the site they set up for Erin?" Evangeline's voice seems to be coming from a great distance.

What are you doing here? What do you want from me? Calla demands silently, but it's already too late. The spirit's presence evaporated as quickly as it materialized.

"Calla?" Evangeline asks clearly.

Calla blinks. "Yeah?"

"Do you want to check Erin's site first?"

"Oh . . . yeah. Sure." She sinks into the chair just vacated by Mason and reaches for the mouse.

The only update on Erin's Web site is that she's been found alive, which is trumpeted in a bold, jubilant headline. A further search of regional newspapers reveals more of the same, as well as the news that the police are hoping to inter-view Erin about her attacker as soon as she's up to it.

"I'm sure they'll find the guy who did it," Evangeline says, hovering over Calla's shoulder. "Or woman. I mean, we don't know it was a guy."

"Yes, we do. Kaitlyn said."

"Oh. Right." Evangeline sighs. "Look, don't worry too much about it."

"Who says I'm worried?"

"You don't have to say it. You look it."

"Okay, I'm worried. What if he comes after me next?"

"How can he? He doesn't even know who you are."

"That reporter found me."

Evangeline falters. "That was a fluke. I'm sure you're safe. Come on. Let's go back out to the porch before it starts snow-ing or something," she adds with forced cheer.

"Wait—can I just check my e-mail for a second?"

"Sure. I'll go get the wine for your grandmother. Be right back."

Left alone, Calla quickly signs in to her screen name, clicks on the mailbox icon. It takes a moment for her to realize she's looking at another e-mail from KZW88@cornell.edu.

Kevin.

Hey, what's up? I was flipping channels on the tv last night and you'll never in a million years believe what popped up. Remember that really stupid movie from 1982 or something, the one we watched at my house that day it was raining and we couldn't go to that clambake at the beach . . . you know, when we both kept saying we couldn't believe we were wasting time watching something so stupid, but we kept thinking it might get better? And it didn't? In fact it got worse and worse and more and more stupid? Well, guess what? It was on again. And I watched the whole thing again. BTW, it's not any better the second time, LOL. Still really really really stupid. So anyway . . . I couldn't believe it was on AGAIN. Much less that I got sucked in AGAIN.

Well, that's my earth-shattering e-mail for today. Write back if you have time. Take care. I hope you're doing okay.

xoxo Kevin

Calla impulsively clicks the Reply button, opening a blank e-mail addressed back to Kevin.

How's this for a coincidence? I saw it too. Last night, I mean. But I had the opposite reaction. I was able to find new and profound meaning in the plot this time around. The symbolism really blew me away. I can't believe you missed it.

JK. I thought it was just as stupid the second time. But yeah, I also watched the whole thing—AGAIN. What does that make us? LOL

It's good to hear from you. I'm hanging in there.

xoxo Calla

"Ready?" Evangeline pokes her head in the door, a glass of wine and two cans of soda balanced in her hands.

141

"Yeah, in a second. I'm just checking my e-mail."

"Anything interesting?" She attempts to push a strand of hair back from her face. Impossible to do without spilling something.

Evangeline spills everything.

"Oh, geez." She looks down at the spreading puddle of wine and Pepsi on the floor. "Am I a klutz, or what?"

"Here, I'll help you. Get paper towels." As she pushes back her chair, she automatically hits Send . . . and immediately wishes she hadn't. Especially since she signed her e-mail with hugs and kisses.

Oh, well. Too late now.

She and Evangeline mop up the floor, gather more wine and soda, and finally make it back out to the porch. There, they find Odelia dozing in her chair, head thrown back, mouth slightly open and making a whistling sound.

"Uh-oh." Calla grins. Odelia can't sit down at night without snoozing.

"Yeah," Ramona says affectionately, "man down."

"Guess it really was past her bedtime," Calla's father comments, and she notices that for someone who's usually pretty shy, he looks surprisingly relaxed, sitting out here with a total stranger.

"Well, we can't let her wine go to waste," Ramona says. "You drink it."

"Why not." He shrugs and accepts the glass.

"I was just telling your dad what a great high school we have," Ramona tells Calla, who promptly decides that if anyone deserves hugs and kisses, it's Evangeline's aunt.

"Yeah, it is a great school," Evangeline promptly speaks up. "The teachers are really challenging, but in a good way. And most of the kids are really cool."

"But not all of them?" Ramona asks wryly.

"Well, Mason goes there, remember?" Evangeline cracks, and even Dad laughs at that.

They talk a little longer about the school, and everything Ramona says is positively glowing. It's almost as though she senses Dad needs some convincing, and is ready to step up to bat on Calla's behalf.

Almost as though?

She *does* know, Calla realizes. And not because Odelia told her, either. Calla never even mentioned this morning's conversation about her going back to California.

Ramona knows because she's, well, psychic. Thank goodness for that. She's doing a hard sell on Lily Dale and Dad is eating it right up.

Later, standing beside the rental car with her father, Calla realizes she isn't ready yet to say good-bye. But he's leaving for the airport early in the morning, so this is it.

"Well," he says, and gestures at the Taggarts' empty porch, where the candle is now extinguished. "That was fun."

"Yeah. You sound surprised."

He shrugs a little, like he's thinking about all that just happened.

Then he says, "Cal, if you really want to stick around here a while longer, maybe even until the end of the year . . . it's okay with me."

Whoa. Maybe Ramona isn't just a psychic, but a witch as well. It sure feels as though Dad has fallen under some kind of magical spell to have done such a quick about-face.

"The end of the year, year? Or the end of the school year?" she asks, trying not to sound too excited. After all, it also means they'll have to be apart for a while longer.

"Maybe both. I just don't know anymore. I'm not crazy about this California situation."

"The job? Or trying to find a place to live?"

"Everything." He shrugs. "I don't know why I didn't realize until just now, tonight, sitting here with your friends, that as much as I miss you and worry about you, you've adjusted incredibly well here in a short time. And it's probably not a good idea to get you involved in another new place when I'm still trying to figure things out myself."

"Figure what out? You mean, *if* you're going to stay there?" she asks, feeling as though she's suddenly reading his mind.

He doesn't want to be there, she realizes. *He's not sure where he wants to be right now, but it isn't there, and it isn't back home in Tampa.*

Poor Dad.

"Where would you go?" she asks. "If you don't finish out the sabbatical, I mean. Back to Florida?"

"I don't know what I'm going to do. But I'll figure things out," he adds with a reassuring nod that doesn't ring true. "Listen, all that matters to me, really, is that *you're* in a good place right now, and that you're surrounded by good people who care about you. Maybe Mom would want you to be here, even . . . I don't know."

"I don't, either." Calla sighs. "There are so many things I wonder about her, and now I'll never have the answers."

"I feel the same way," Dad says, wearing such a cryptic expression that Calla realizes he, too, is searching. Maybe not for the same thing she's trying to find, but Mom's death left him with questions, too.

"You knew her better than anyone, though, Dad."

He shakes his head. "I used to think that. But . . . I wonder."

"I guess that's what happens when people die. We look back and—"

"No, not just after she died. I wondered while she was alive, too." It's not like him to speak so freely to Calla.

Maybe it's the dark, or the wine, or the laid-back mood that lingers from the Taggarts' porch.

In any case, Dad goes on. "Last spring wasn't the greatest time."

Yeah, tell me about it, Calla thinks, remembering her breakup with Kevin.

But of course, that's not what Dad's talking about.

"I was getting ready for this sabbatical," he says, almost like he's thinking out loud, to himself, "and Mom was wrapped up in her work, as usual, and . . . things were tense."

"You mean, between you and Mom?"

"I shouldn't even be telling you this. I don't even know why I am. Except . . . it's been on my mind, and who else am I going to tell?"

"So, were you guys, like, fighting a lot?" Calla asks, thinking back. She was so caught up in her own problems back then. "I remember Mom not wanting to take time off from work to go to California."

"No, not fighting so much. I mean, we argued—everyone argues. But your mother was starting to become . . . detached. That's the only way I can explain it. It was like she'd taken a big step back—from me, anyway. And now I wonder if . . ."

"If what?"

"Never mind," Dad says quietly. "I don't know what's wrong with me tonight."

I wish there were a way to know what was going on with Mom before she died, Calla thinks, frustrated. But her secrets died with her. It's not like she kept a diary or wrote letters or—

Wait a minute. Of course!

Mom might not have left an actual paper trail, but she might have left a record somewhere else.

Before Calla can blurt anything to her father, he shakes his head abruptly and gets into the car. "I've got to get going. It's late and I've got an early flight in the morning."

"I know . . ." Calla's thoughts whirl. Should she even suggest it? Would it upset him further?

He reaches out and turns the key in the ignition. "You've got to get to bed and so do I."

They hug each other fiercely.

"I'll come back to visit again in a few weeks," he promises before driving away, leaving Calla with a major lump in her throat.

Lurking in the dense growth of shrubs outside the yellow brick building that houses the community theater, he watches people trickle out to the parking lot.

Voices call out cheerful goodnights, car doors slam, engines start.

Hayley Gorzynski has yet to appear.

Tense, he waits, making sure to stay well out of the glare each time an arc of headlights swings past on the way to the street. His breath puffs smoky white in the cold night air.

There's supposed to be a first frost by morning. Erin Shannahan wouldn't have survived this, he thinks in frustration.

Renewed anger ignites inside him just as the theater doors burst open one last time.

Sure enough, a pretty blond emerges, flanked by a middle-aged woman and a lanky dark-haired kid he recognizes as the boy who's playing Danny Zuko. All three of them are carrying what look like scripts, the woman's attached to a clipboard.

"So if you can both stay late after rehearsal tomorrow night," the woman is saying, "we can go over that dance scene until we get it right. I know the choreography is tricky."

"She's got it down," the kid says. "I'm the one who's having a hard time."

"You're doing great. We just need to practice together, that's all. We'll be fine by opening night." That's Hayley's voice, sweet and melodious.

He wonders what it would sound like pleading for her life. Or screaming.

You'll find out soon enough, he promises himself. *Meanwhile, there's that other problem to take care of.*

Yes. It's about time for a road trip.

TWELVE

Monday, September 10
12:51 p.m.

Seeing Dad was great, but on Monday morning, Calla is glad to get back to the routine of school.

The old brick building already feels familiar, and she's getting the hang of the daily rhythm here already. When she saw Willow this morning, she offered to help Calla again with math, tomorrow night. She said she can't do tonight because she takes a class in the Dale. She didn't say what kind of class, but Calla figures it's much more likely to be in metaphysics than, say, gymnastics.

It was Calla's turn to be team captain in gym, so she picked Kasey first and was rewarded with a smile and an invitation to eat lunch together.

She said she'd try, not sure what to do about Willow and Sarita.

In the end, though, it doesn't matter. She finds Jacy waiting for her, leaning against the wall outside the door to the cafeteria. At least, he seems to be waiting for her, because the moment he sees her, he straightens and says, "Come on. Come with me."

"Where are we going?"

"Outside. For a walk."

She wants to point out that they're not allowed to leave the school during lunch period. But then, he knows that. He just doesn't care.

Does *she*?

Not enough to tell Jacy to go without her.

He leads the way down a flight of back stairs past the janitor's rooms, then out a door that opens onto the athletic field, behind the bleachers.

The day is breezy, and the golden September sun shines brightly overhead. Calla, dressed in a short-sleeved top and a cute, summery skirt, wishes she had a coat.

"Here," Jacy says, and shrugs out of his own jean jacket as they cross the grassy meadow alongside the track. He hands it to her.

"Oh, I'm okay."

"You're cold. Take it."

She *is* cold. She slips it on and is enveloped in the clean, unfamiliar masculine scent of him. This is what it would be like if she were in his arms, she decides. Well, almost.

And she really hopes he doesn't know what she's thinking.

They quickly reach the dappled shade of the woods on the far side of the field. A narrow path cuts through the brush, and Jacy follows it so easily she can tell he's done it dozens of times.

"Is this where you come when you skip lunch?" she asks, her voice hushed because it seems necessary here. Almost as though this is some kind of sacred place.

"Sometimes I come here," Jacy says with a shrug. "No one else is ever around, so I like it."

She nods. If he were any other guy, she might think he was trying to get her alone in the woods so he could make a move on her.

Not Jacy. Which is almost too bad, because despite how badly she wants to talk to him, she honestly wouldn't mind his making a move on her, either.

It's cooler in the woods, and the air smells of moist, damp earth and decomposing leaves.

For a split second, Calla thinks of poor Erin Shannahan, lying for days in a remote forest, left for dead.

Then she thinks of the nameless, faceless person who did that to her—and how he's still out there somewhere—and her stomach churns. Dizzy enough to stop walking for a moment, she gulps a deep breath to steady her nerves.

Jacy doesn't seem to notice. He's up ahead, stopping and pointing to a massive fallen tree.

"This is a good spot," he decides as she catches up. "Want to sit?"

"Sure." She lowers herself onto the moss-covered log after checking only briefly to make sure she's not about to sit on anything wet or muddy or . . . alive.

"It's clean," he says, and she looks up to see him watching her, almost looking amused.

"Oh, I don't care about that. It's just . . . I'm used to Florida. There, I'd be worried about poisonous snakes and spiders."

"We have a few of those here. Poison ivy, too," Jacy tells her, and she gingerly moves her bare lower legs out of the foliage.

"Which one do you want?" Jacy holds out a couple of brown bags. "One is peanut butter and jelly. The other is peanut butter and honey—we ran out of jelly."

"It's okay. I'm not big on jelly." She takes the bag he offers her, deciding not to tell him she's not big on honey, either. "Thanks."

"You're welcome." He sits beside her, takes out his own sandwich and takes a bite.

Calla unwraps hers, finding it touching—and yeah, kind of romantic—that he actually thought to bring her a lunch. In the bag are a bottle of water, a napkin, and an apple.

She'd probably actually be hungry if she weren't so caught off guard about being alone here with him—and so expectant about whatever it is he's going to say.

She takes a small bite and listens to the birds chirp overhead, wishing he would talk.

He doesn't seem to be in any hurry, though. Nor does he seem to mind the silence.

She wonders if he did, after all, bring her here to talk. Maybe not. Maybe he just thought it would be nice to have a picnic.

"I think you're right."

She looks up, startled. And confused. Did she miss something?

"Right about what?" she asks.

"Your mother."

At those words, the hunk of sandwich turns to paste in her mouth and she has to gulp water to get it down.

"What do you mean?" she asks Jacy, her heart beating so loudly she's sure he must hear it.

"I think that something happened to your mother. And I'm sure Darrin's visit had something to do with it."

She nods slowly. "What about Aiyana?"

"She's your guide," Jacy says simply.

"My spirit guide? How do you know?"

"I meditated on it. I asked my own guides. And that's the answer I got," he says, as though that's an everyday thing. "Have you seen her lately?"

"At Evangeline's the other night—I caught a glimpse of her."

"What was going on? When she appeared, I mean."

"Oh, nothing, really. Evangeline was making her brother get off the computer so I could use it. Aiyana popped up out of nowhere, but only for a few seconds."

"And that was it? That was the only time you've seen her, aside from what you told me the other day?"

Remembering the disembodied hug by the lake on Saturday morning, she hesitates. Then she says, "Yes. That was it."

After all, she has no idea if it was Aiyana who hugged her, or her mother, or . . .

Well, for all she knows, it could have been some other spirit.

What Jacy asked is whether she's *seen* Aiyana any other time, and the answer to that is definitely no.

"If you think Aiyana is trying to tell me something about my mom's death, what am I supposed to do about it?" Calla asks Jacy, feeling helpless. "I mean, I can't go to the police in Tampa and tell them a spirit is telling me they need to look into what happened to her. I don't have any proof."

"No. You don't."

She thinks of the idea she had the other night and wonders if her mother might, indeed, have left some proof after all. But there's no way of knowing that yet.

It's a good idea to keep that on the back burner for now.

"What am I supposed to do?" she asks Jacy, deciding not to mention that to him, either.

"Start by finding out where Darrin is now."

"How?"

"His parents still live in Lily Dale."

"And you want me to . . . what? Knock on their door and ask them where their son is?"

"It's a start."

"I can't do that," Calla protests.

"Sure, you can." He pauses. "I'll go with you."

"You will?" She considers that. "When?"

He shrugs. "Whenever you want."

She nods slowly. "Okay. I'll think about it. But . . . I have to figure out if I'm ready to do that."

"I know."

She smiles faintly. "You know an awful lot about me."

Jacy tilts his head, and his expression is serious.

"Yeah," is all he says, and she gets the impression he knows more about her, in some ways, than she knows about herself.

———

Walking down the empty hall at school, Calla wishes her science teacher had asked someone else to go up to the media center to pick up some handouts. Still playing catch-up, she was planning to spend the five-minute break the teacher just gave them to go over her notes from last week.

Oh, well. It does feel good to stretch her legs a little. Spending lunch hour outside with Jacy sparked some hint of cabin fever this afternoon.

Her footsteps echoing down the corridor, Calla turns the corner and stops short just outside the auditorium, startled by the sudden, jaunty sound of a piano playing inside.

Someone is singing. A girl's melodious soprano.

She recognizes the song after a moment: "Hopelessly Devoted to You." Olivia Newton-John sang it in the movie *Grease* with John Travolta. Calla watched it with her mother whenever they caught it on television. Mom said it was one of her favorite movies when she was a kid.

Unable to resist a peek, she slips into the back of the auditorium to see who's singing.

To her shock, the cavernous space is dark. Deserted. Silent.

The piano bench is empty, lid closed.

And the music stopped as suddenly as if someone had turned off a radio. Maybe that's all it was. Only . . .

There's no radio that she can see, and it really sounded as if someone were rehearsing live music in here.

Spooked, Calla backs out of the auditorium and hurries toward the media center, wondering if the school might be as haunted as Lily Dale itself.

It's been another long day, and Calla is relieved when the last bell rings as Mr. Bombeck is in the midst of working a difficult problem on the board. She has no clue what he's doing. Her thoughts keep drifting to what happened earlier, in the auditorium.

It's probably no big deal—just a random haunting—but for some reason, that ghostly music left her with a lingering feeling of, well, doom. As if that makes any sense at all. "Hopelessly Devoted to You" might be a melancholy song, but it's not a funeral march.

"All right. We'll save this equation for tomorrow," Mr. Bombeck announces above the immediately chattering voices and scraping chairs. "Calla? Can you please stay for a minute and see me?"

She sighs inwardly and approaches Mr. Bombeck's desk as the room clears out and the hall beyond fills with voices and lockers slamming.

"Have a seat." Mr. Bombeck closes the door and gestures at the chair beside his desk.

She sits. So does he.

He looks intently at her, steepling his fingers beneath his chin as if he's about to pray. "Were you able to follow today's lesson, Calla?"

"Pretty much," she responds, trying to put her other concerns out of her head.

"You seemed a little lost."

Oh, yeah, that's just because every time I turn around, I'm seeing and hearing ghosts, she wants to say. *Other than that, no problem.*

"How about if we take a few minutes to go over what we did today?" he asks, reaching for the chalk. "And I'll give you some worksheets. You can meet with Willow again tonight or tomorrow, and hopefully, you'll be getting up to speed by the end of the week."

She nods, deciding not to mention that Willow has a homecoming committee meeting tonight. She has a feeling Mr. Bombeck won't consider that a good reason not to meet with her study partner and do homework.

Twenty minutes later, Mr. Bombeck lets her go at last. She hurries through the almost-empty corridors to her locker.

"There you are!" Evangeline calls as Calla walks toward her. "I was just about to leave, but I didn't want to walk home without you."

"Sorry . . . I had to stay after for math."

"I know. I saw Jacy and I know he's in your last period so I asked him where you were. Any excuse to talk to him, right?" she adds with a wry smile.

Calla smiles back, hoping it doesn't look too forced. She gathers her things from her locker as her friend changes the subject to homecoming.

"I heard Russell Lancione is going to ask me to go with him," Evangeline says. "I don't know if I want him to. I mean, it would be nice to go to the dance, but . . . maybe not with Russell."

"Why not?" Calla asks, even though she knows the answer will probably have something to do with Jacy.

Evangeline shrugs. "He's nice and everything, but . . . you know . . . he's . . ."

Not Jacy, Calla thinks, seeing her friend's wistful expression. *Yeah, I totally hear you.*

But Evangeline says only, "He's just kind of blah."

Calla grins. "I guess blah isn't your type, huh?"

"I guess not. What about you?"

"Blah's not my type, either."

Evangeline laughs. "No, I mean, what about you and the homecoming dance?"

For a split second, Calla wonders if Evangeline possibly read her mind and knows that she, too, is longing for Jacy to ask her.

"Nobody's asked you yet, right?"

Oh. Phew.

"No . . . why?" Calla slams her locker door closed and pulls on her jacket.

"I probably shouldn't say anything, but . . ."

"But what?" Calla prods, as they head toward the exit.

"I heard Blue's going to ask you to homecoming."

Calla's jaw drops. "Who said that?"

"Linda Samuels, this girl who goes out with Ryan Kruger, told me. She said Blue's thinking about it."

"Really?" *Then why is he sending e-mails to Willow York about the homecoming dance? Is he planning to ask her first, and I'm just the backup in case she says no?*

"Don't tell him I said that, though," Evangeline says.

"Oh, please. As if." Calla laughs and shakes her head.

No way is she going to get her hopes up that Blue will ask her.

Still, as she and Evangeline head toward home, despite

everything she's been through, Calla finds her heart a little lighter for the first time all day. Thinking about a school dance—even if part of it is worrying about who may or may not ask her—feels welcome and normal compared to dwelling on ghosts and death, as she has been.

THIRTEEN

Tuesday, September 11
7:39 a.m.

The next morning, Calla steps out onto the porch with her backpack to find Lily Dale draped in heavy gray fog. The air feels like a warm, wet blanket and a dank smell is coming from the lakefront. Oh, ick. What a change from yesterday's crisp, sunny weather. All that's missing is the gloomy sound of a foghorn and a clanking bell.

"Gross out, isn't it?" Evangeline calls as she heads down the steps next door with her own backpack. They've already got their morning timing perfectly in sync.

"I never know what to expect around here," Calla says as they fall into step together, heading toward the gate though they can't see more than a few feet in front of them. "I thought it was supposed to be nice out today."

"Where'd you hear that?"

"The weatherman on the news last night."

"Oh, please." Evangeline dismisses that with a wave of her hand. "Around here, it's impossible to predict. Did you ever hear what Mark Twain said about the weather in western New York? He used to live around here, you know."

"No, I didn't know. What did he say?"

"If you don't like the weather, wait five minutes."

Calla smiles. "Yeah, no kid—" She breaks off abruptly, startled to glimpse a familiar figure just ahead in the mist.

Kaitlyn.

"What's wrong?" Evangeline asks.

Kaitlyn is shaking her head ominously, just as before.

"Stop him!"

Her words shriek through Calla's brain and then she disappears, enveloped in fog.

"It was Kaitlyn," she tells Evangeline shakily. "She wants me to stop him."

"Still?" Evangeline grabs her hand and squeezes it. "Breathe. You look like you're going to faint."

"How am I supposed to stop him if I don't know who or where he is?"

"I think it's time," Evangeline says slowly, "that you sat in on one of my beginning mediumship classes. You need to learn how to develop your abilities. I know you're going to say you can't, and come up with a million excuses, but—"

"Okay."

There's a pause. "Okay?" Evangeline looks confused. "Okay, what?"

"Okay. I'll come to one of your classes. This is crazy. If

I'm going to do this sort of thing—and it really seems like I don't have a choice—then I'm going to do it right."

"Hey . . . what are you doing all by your lonesome?"

Munching on an apple, Calla looks up from her book to see Blue standing over her. "Oh, hi. I'm trying to read Shakespeare. *Hamlet*."

"For pleasure?"

"Are you kidding? For English." And she's read the same page at least three times just now, preoccupied with her decision to accompany Evangeline to a class. Evangeline thinks her Saturday-morning instructor will let Calla sit in.

"We're reading *King Lear* in my section," Blue comments. "I'd rather do *Hamlet*. We did it in my old school, so at least I know it."

His old school, Calla knows, is a fancy boarding school he attended until he got kicked out. He didn't tell her why, and she hasn't felt comfortable asking, but she's definitely curious.

Grabbing a chair from the next table and straddling it backward, he asks, "So, where are your friends today?"

"Oh, you mean Willow and Sarita?"

He nods.

"They had to go to the computer lab to work on a flyer for the homecoming dance."

"Oh. That. Is that the only thing they ever think about?" he asks with a good-natured roll of his blue eyes.

She's spared having to answer, because a wadded up ball of paper sails through the air and hits Blue on the head.

"Hey!" He looks around to see his friend Ryan, the obvious culprit, beckoning him from two tables away.

"Looks like you're being summoned," Calla observes.

"Yeah. I'll let you get back to your Shakespeare. See you later."

Watching him walk away, Calla can feel the curious attention from a group of girls sitting at the end of her table.

Sure enough, moments after she goes back to her reading—or pretends to—one of them comes walking over. She's a petite blond, just short of pretty thanks to close-set eyes and a narrow, pointy nose.

"Hi," she says. "You're the new girl, right? From Florida?"

"Right. Calla."

"I'm Pam."

"Nice to meet you," she says politely.

"Are you seeing him?"

"Who?" Calla asks, knowing darn well who.

"Blue Slayton."

"We've gone out," Calla admits.

"Really? Are you guys going to homecoming together?"

"I don't know . . . I mean, no. Not that I know of." Officially feeling like a tongue-tied idiot, she shrugs and wishes Pam would go away.

"Want to come over and sit with us?"

Normally, Calla would welcome the invitation, but she really isn't in the mood to field curious questions about Blue and homecoming.

Still, maybe it's better than sitting here alone with *Hamlet*.

"Sure," she tells Pam. "Let me just get my stuff together and I'll come right down. Thanks."

It can't hurt to make some new cafeteria friends, she decides as she sticks a straw wrapper into her Shakespeare text as a bookmark. After all, who knows if Willow will want to sit with her after this?

Why wouldn't she? Because you were talking to Blue? Isn't that a little extreme?

She wonders if Blue would even have come over if Calla had been sitting with Willow as usual. Probably not, if he's sending Willow e-mails about homecoming.

It's being held in October, kicked off with a pep rally after school, then the big varsity football game against the school's archrivals, the Brocton Bulldogs. Afterward is the formal dance in the gym, with a live band this year instead of the usual DJ.

Calla keeps telling herself it's no big deal if she doesn't get to go. After all, she's new here and it's not like it's a prom.

Prom. Hah.

Last spring, Kevin dumped her right before her junior prom. She wound up going—just as friends—with Paul Horton, who's an inch shorter than her on a regular day. He was a good three inches shorter on prom night because of the heels she'd picked out when she thought she was going with Kevin. She stubbornly decided to keep the shoes since they went perfectly with the dress, and suffer through looking down at the top of her date's head all night. Maybe deep down, she was thinking that at the last minute, Paul would uninvite her . . . and Kevin would simultaneously reappear in her life.

So much for that.

As for Lily Dale's homecoming dance, she can't help dwelling on that e-mail she saw and wondering if Willow is going with Blue despite being broken up and despite Evangeline hearing he's going to ask Calla.

She wonders, too—even though it's ridiculous—whether there's the slightest chance Jacy might ask her to go with him.

If he does—not that he will—what would you do about Evangeline?

It doesn't matter, she tells herself as she walks over to join Pam and her friends. *Because Jacy won't ask you. Period.*

When Calla walks into the house after babysitting at Paula's, she moodily lets the door slam shut after her.

"Calla? Is that you?"

"Yeah."

She spent the rest of her lunch period wishing she had stuck to Shakespeare. Pam and her friends were gossipy, and Calla was turned off by mean-spirited comments a few of them made about poor Donald Reamer.

Later, she failed a quiz in Bombeck's class, and Paula's kids insisted on playing Candyland for two hours straight. Moving around and around the tedious game board was about as much fun as taking the pop quiz in math. Dylan insisted on an extra game piece for Kelly—who, Calla is starting to believe, might be nothing more than an imaginary friend after all. It's not as if she herself has sensed a presence lingering around Dylan, or as if Kelly's game piece moved itself around the board, which might have been a heck of a lot faster. Instead, Dylan did it, taking an extra and painstaking turn each round, so that the game lasted far longer than it should have.

Home at last, Calla heads right for the stairs. She'd love to flop onto her bed and read or listen to music. That's not going to happen, though. She has a pile of homework to do.

"Come in here," Odelia calls from the back of the house. "I have something to show you."

"What is it?" Calla drapes her backpack and jacket over the newel post and heads to the kitchen.

The room is empty . . . or so she thinks.

Then she hears Odelia's voice again, coming from under the kitchen table.

"Gammy?" Calla bends over to see her grandmother on all fours. "Are you okay? Did you drop something?"

"She jumped off my lap when the door slammed. See her?"

"Who, Miriam?"

"No!" A laugh spills from under the table. "The kitten. I picked her up from Andy's house this afternoon."

"Oh!" Calla peers into the dim space beneath the table. "Where is she?"

"Back there, see? Here, kitty kitty kitty," Odelia says in a high-pitched voice. "It's okay, you can come out now. This is Calla. She's nice."

Calla finally spots a tiny gray ball of fur and a pair of glittering eyes on the far side of the table, cowering between the table leg and one of the chairs. "Oh! Look at her . . . she's so sweet!"

"She is, isn't she?" Odelia grunts, rubbing the small of her back. "I can't stay down here like this. See if you can get her out, will you?"

As her grandmother backs her hefty form out from under the table and stands with a loud groan, Calla inches forward. "Here, kitty. Come here, little kitty."

To her surprise, the tiny creature darts toward her. Calla scoops her into her arms, then quickly ducks out and stands. "Gotcha!"

The kitten cuddles in her arms, blinking up at her.

"Wow," Calla says. "I think I'm in love. Is she the most precious thing ever, or what?"

"She is that. What should we name her?"

"She looks like a Gert to me," Calla says promptly.

"Gert? As in Gertrude?"

"Don't you think?"

Odelia smiles. "Gert it is. How'd you come up with that?"

Calla shrugs. "Sometimes things just pop into my head."

Odelia looks thoughtfully at her. "Speaking of that . . . we should talk about—"

"I have a pile of homework to do," Calla interrupts, knowing what Odelia is going to say, and not wanting to get into it now. "And I really need to keep my grades up while I'm here, or, you know . . . Dad will make me leave."

"Okay. No rush. Your schoolwork comes first. I just know that things are happening to you here—things you can't possibly understand. I remember when I was your age, trying to deal with my gifts and being scared out of my mind."

Calla's hand goes still on the kitten's soft fur as she contemplates that. She never really wondered what it must have been like for Odelia, coming to terms with her visions of dead people. She just figured her grandmother always took it for granted, the way she does now.

She was once in my shoes, Calla realizes. She gets it.

But what about the whole Kaitlyn Riggs thing? Her grandmother already told her it was wrong for her to get involved in the first place. Remembering Odelia's reaction to Mrs. Riggs's visit last week, she knows that her grandmother would freak if she knew about the call from that reporter, much less about Kaitlyn's visits, and Calla getting caught up in the Erin Shannahan case.

Which she isn't . . . yet. Not officially, anyway.

What if the killer strikes again . . . and again?

Stop him!

All she has to do is hang on until that class on Saturday, and maybe she can figure out if there's a way to use her psychic abilities to zero in on the killer.

"Oh!" Odelia slaps her forehead. "I almost forgot to tell you two things. One is, you got some mail today. I put it on the desk in the other room. The other thing is, I have a message for you."

"From Spirit?" Calla braces herself. Maybe Kaitlyn Riggs has been visiting Odelia, too.

But her grandmother laughs. Hard. Then she says, "No, not from Spirit. From Blue Slayton. And he used the good old-fashioned telephone to get through."

"Really?" Calla breaks into a grin, wondering if Evangeline was right and he's going to ask her to homecoming.

"Really," her grandmother assures her. "He called after school."

"Really?"

"Really," Odelia repeats again, with a smile. "Oh, but can you hold off on calling him back until after I order us a pizza for dinner? I was so busy with Gert here that I didn't have time to cook."

"Sure. Here, give her to me. I'll play with her."

As her grandmother goes to find the takeout menu and the phone, Calla brings the kitten into the living room. So Blue called her. Does he want to ask her to homecoming? Maybe that's what he was about to do when Ryan hit him in the head with that stupid wad of paper.

On the desk, she finds an envelope addressed to her in Lisa's loopy handwriting.

"What do you think this is?" she asks the kitten, balancing her with one hand while she opens the envelope with the other.

Inside is an airline voucher. A yellow Post-it note is stuck to it.

Calla, All yours. Let me know when to meet you at the airport! Love, Lisa.

Smiling, she puts the voucher back into the envelope and tucks it into the top drawer. She'll use it at some point. Just not yet.

The kitten squirms in her arms.

"What? You want to get down? Want to play? Okay." Calla sets her gently on the floor.

Odelia keeps several skeins of yarn in a basket by her chair, along with several needles, though she doesn't knit or crochet . . . yet. She says she always wanted to learn and wants to be ready with supplies when she finally gets around to it. Just as she has a guitar she's never learned to play, and keeps a bin full of scrapbooking supplies for the day she feels like, as she put it, "sorting through and organizing a lifetime's worth of junk." Typical Odelia—creative and chaotic, Calla thinks with a smile.

She tosses a ball of yellow yarn across the floor, holding on to one end. Gert trips over her little paws as she scrambles to play with it, and Calla can't help but giggle.

A few minutes later, Odelia reappears and holds out the cordless phone. "Pizza is on its way," she says. "Half anchovy and pineapple for me, half mushroom and pepperoni for you."

"Perfect." They've been getting pizza at least once a week. So far, she's refused to try Odelia's unusual combo, unconvinced that it's as yummy as she claims.

"Calla, can you keep the kitten occupied for a while so that I can get a few things done around here? I've been distracted by her all afternoon."

Calla thinks of all the homework she's supposed to be doing.

Then she thinks of the call from Blue, and her conversation with Jacy today, and the math test she failed, and the endless rounds of Candyland.

"Sure," she tells her grandmother, "I'd love to play with her. Just . . . I have to call Blue first."

"Are you going out with him again?"

"Saturday night."

"Oh . . . I have a message circle that night down in Sinclairville."

"It's okay. I don't think he was planning on inviting you to come along like Dad did," Calla says lightly, and grins at her.

Odelia laughs. "Very funny. Do you need his phone number, or do you have it memorized already?"

"I need it."

"555-4782," recites Odelia, who was a close friend of

Blue's father, David Slayton—"before he went Hollywood," as she put it.

She starts to leave the room as Calla dials, though she seems to be taking her sweet old time, stopping to straighten a couple of picture frames and plump sofa pillows along the way.

Ha, that's what Mom used to do when she wanted to eavesdrop on Calla's calls to Kevin, back when their relationship was in full swing . . . back when Mom was alive.

Suddenly, Calla finds herself overwhelmed by grief that hits hard, seemingly out of nowhere.

Oh, Mom. Her eyes are swimming with hot tears, her gut aching so that she's almost doubled over.

Why does it happen this way? It's not that she ever really forgets about her loss. There's a baseline of sadness every day, but then out of the blue, something triggers a fierce tide of sorrow and longing that sweeps her right over the edge.

What she wouldn't give to be in her own living room back in Tampa right now, talking to Kevin, with Mom annoying her by trying to listen—

"Hello?"

Calla jumps at the unexpected voice in her ear, having forgotten, for a split second, just whom she'd dialed or that she was even on the phone.

"Um . . . Blue?" Her voice comes out sounding a little strangled.

"Yeah. Calla?"

"Yeah. Hi." She wipes a sleeve across her wet eyes.

"Hang on for a second, will you? I'm on the other line."

With Willow? Calla wonders as he clicks off. Or some other girl?

170

She glumly throws the yarn across the floor again, expecting a long wait, but he's back on the line before Gert has even skidded to a stop at the fuzzy yellow ball.

"Sorry about that. So, remember how we changed our date to this Saturday night?" he asks, and her heart sinks. He's not going to ask her to homecoming. He's going to blow her off entirely.

"My dad gave me these tickets," he tells her, "to this concert in Buffalo, and I thought we could go. But only if you like jazz."

She knows nothing about jazz. She's surprised that he does. And boy, is she relieved that he isn't canceling on her.

"Sure," she says. "That sounds great."

"I'll pick you up at six. Okay?"

"Okay."

"Good. See you at lunch tomorrow?"

"Yup." Calla smiles as she hangs up the phone. "Guess what, Gert? I think he likes me."

The cat stops pawing at the ball and looks up solemnly.

"Yeah," Calla tells her, "I do like him, too. But don't worry. I won't let myself get hurt. Not this time."

Again, she thinks of Kevin, and wishes she had never answered his e-mail.

FOURTEEN

Wednesday, September 12
3:40 p.m.

Okay, Calla probably shouldn't have postponed her homework last night, though romping around on the floor with Gert and a ball of yarn was the best time she's had in ages.

Unfortunately, she rushed through her homework, and it showed. She wasn't doing as poorly in her other subjects as she has been in math, but thanks to pure carelessness, she has to rewrite her social studies essay on top of reading both last night and tonight's *Hamlet* assignments for English. She had to fake her way through the class discussion today.

But that was better than math, where Mr. Bombeck handed back her homework covered in red ink slashes and grimly told her to redo it by tomorrow, in addition to the new assignment. Luckily she's working with Willow tonight.

Another glitch, though: she's going to need the Internet in order to research a science project that will be assigned in the next few weeks. That will mean staying after school to use it there, and skipping a couple of days working at Paula's, or asking to use Ramona's after she gets home. Knowing Mason and Evangeline hog it nightly as it is, she hates to ask.

Then again, she does have that glimmer of an idea she back-burnered earlier.

One that might give her access to more than just the Internet.

But does she dare pursue it with her father?

Meanwhile, she'll probably be up until midnight, catching up on everything after she gets back from Willow's later. *Unless I can get something done here,* she tells herself as she climbs the steps to Paula's porch after school.

Maybe she can settle the boys in front of a video and—

Nah. That wouldn't be fair. Paula can do that herself. She's paying Calla to entertain the boys, and that's what she needs to do.

"Come on in," Paula calls in response to her knock.

Calla finds her in the living room, reading a book called *Love You Forever* to the boys, who are curled up on either side of her.

"We've been to the library, and we're reading our way through the stack. I'll finish this one," Paula says, looking up from the book. "Have a seat."

Calla does, and finds herself drawn into the whimsical story, which is about a mother who continues to rock her child to sleep with a lullaby through every stage of his life. Calla is teary eyed when it concludes with the grown son cradling his elderly mother in his arms, rocking her to sleep with the same lullaby.

As she sneaks a hand up to wipe her moist cheeks, she catches Paula doing the same thing. Maybe she, too, lost her mom. Or maybe it's just because she is a mom. Whatever . . . when she looks up, her eyes are shiny, and she smiles at Calla.

"That one gets me every time," she tells her.

"Can you read it to us, Calla?" Dylan asks. "I want to hear it again."

"Oh, let Calla read a different one. How about a silly one?" Paula speaks up quickly, as if she knows that anything that tugs on the heartstrings—especially anything involving a mother and child—is especially emotional for her right now.

"You can read *Walter the Farting Dog,* then," Dylan decides.

"Fart!" Ethan echoes.

"Oh, for Pete's sake. They're all yours, Calla." With a laugh, Paula pulls herself to standing and hobbles toward the kitchen. In the doorway, she turns back. "Oh, I almost forgot to tell you . . . someone was asking about you down at the café this morning."

"What do you mean?"

"My husband was on his way out, and he overheard a man who wanted to know if there was a new girl in town, about seventeen, a medium who was living with her grandmother. You're the only one around here who fits the bill."

"Who was the man?" Calla asks, remembering the AP reporter who called. And Kaitlyn's killer.

Please let it have been the reporter. Please.

"Marty had never seen him before. And he said he had sunglasses on, so he couldn't really see his face."

"Did the guy get my name?"

"I don't know. Unlike me, my husband is the type of person who doesn't like to get involved, so he left." She rolls her eyes. "You know, if I were there, I would have gone over and asked who he was and why he was asking about you. When Marty told me . . . I don't know. It made me nervous and—" Paula glances at Dylan and breaks off abruptly.

Calla looks over to see that the little boy's eyes are round.

"That was the bad man," he says suddenly. "Right?"

"What are you talking about, honey?" Paula asks.

"The man. The one with the raccoon eye. Kelly told me he's looking for Calla."

"Dylan was with your husband when he was in the café?" Calla asks Paula, shaken.

"No. He was here with me." Paula looks at her son. "You didn't see the man today, Dylan. You weren't with Daddy."

"No, Kelly told me about him last night, Mommy. When I was in my bed."

Paula smiles tightly. "Maybe you just had a bad dream."

Calla can't seem to find her voice at all. Her pulse is racing.

"He's a real bad guy, not a bad dream guy," Dylan insists, "and he's here, and Kelly says he's going to get Calla."

Paula looks helplessly at her. "Sorry. He must have heard me talking to Marty."

Calla nods, not buying that for a second.

Dylan's father is a medium. It's hereditary.

He knows, she thinks, watching the child, who is scowling now and flipping the pages of a library book. *He knows things, like I do. Maybe Kelly is his spirit guide and—*

"Calla?" Ethan cuts into her thoughts, thrusting a book at her. "*Walter*?"

She forces a smile. "Sure, Ethan. I'll read the *Walter* book."

Paula's comment—and Dylan's ominous warning—cast a major pall over Calla's afternoon. As she trudges up the path toward her grandmother's front steps, her legs brushing against an overgrown hodgepodge of late summer flowers in full bloom, she's still not quite sure what to make of any of it.

"Calla!"

She turns, startled, and spots Evangeline waving from the porch next door, where she's curled up with a textbook.

"Hey, got a minute? Or are you busy?"

"Supposedly." Evangeline snaps the book closed. "But anything's better than conjugating French verbs. What's up?"

Calla makes a beeline for the porch, needing to get an expert opinion on what happened at Paula's. She quickly explains, and Evangeline tilts her head as she digests the information for a long, thoughtful moment.

"The thing is, Calla, little boys have active imaginations. Especially Dylan."

"I know. He has an imaginary friend." *Or so he says.* "And, I mean, the other day, he decided he was a superhero and wore a dish towel tucked into the back of his T-shirt all afternoon. He wouldn't talk to me unless I called him Captain the Brave."

Evangeline smiles. "See? The kid definitely lives in a fantasy world. He probably overheard his parents talking about some guy who was snooping around here looking for you, and turned him into a bad guy."

176

"Yeah. That's what I keep trying to tell myself." Calla hesitates. "The only thing is, Paula said Marty just overheard that comment today, but Dylan said Kelly told him about it last night."

"So what? He's a little kid. They don't keep track of time. He's just confused."

"I guess." She shrugs. "What really matters is that someone was looking for me. Right? Which is freaking me out a little. Okay . . . a lot."

"It was probably just another reporter."

"But what if Dylan really did have some kind of premonition?"

"Come on, Calla." Evangeline touches her arm reassuringly. "Even then, so what? What are the odds that it's not just some snooping reporter?"

"Why would Dylan call a reporter a bad guy, though?"

Evangeline snorts at that. "Because not everyone likes reporters. Look at the paparazzi. They're really nosy, and brazen, and—"

"And Dylan is five," Calla points out. "What does he know about the paparazzi? You're really stretching it, Evangeline."

"I know. I'm trying to make you feel better. Guess it's not working?"

"Guess not," she says flatly, wishing she could snap out of this dark anxiety.

"Just hang in there until Saturday morning. You'll come to my class with me, and you'll learn how to meditate and—"

"Meditate? Evangeline, how's that really going to help me? Dylan said the man is *dangerous*. That he wants to hurt me, and—"

The front door creaks open. She promptly clamps her mouth shut and looks up to see Evangeline's aunt framed in the doorway.

"Dinner's read— Oh . . . Hi, Calla." Ramona peers more closely at her. "Are you okay?"

"I'm fine. Why?"

"You're not fine."

Calla and Evangeline exchange a glance.

"What makes you say that?" Calla asks Ramona, who shrugs.

Okay, stupid question. *Duh. She's a psychic, remember?*

"Want to talk about it?"

"No thanks," Calla says quickly. "I'm good. Really."

Not really.

But Ramona and Paula are friends. Calla doesn't want Ramona to let Paula know how rattled Calla is by what Paula, and Dylan, said. Because, really, it's probably no big deal. Her overactive imagination is just trying to make it into one.

Or maybe your own sixth sense is telling you something is wrong, a little voice whispers.

"Well if you change your mind . . ."

"Yeah. Thanks, Ramona." Turning to Evangeline and wishing they could have finished their conversation, Calla says, "See you in the morning."

"Oh, wait, Calla?" Ramona stops her as she turns to leave. "Before I forget, I talked to your grandmother earlier about taking you with Evangeline and me when we go to the mall one day next week. I was thinking you might want to shop for some new outfits, maybe stop in at the salon for a haircut, my treat. Want to come?"

"Do you really have to ask? Of course she does!" Evangeline answers for her. "Right, Calla?"

Actually, shopping and salons are the last thing on her mind right now.

Then again, she does have babysitting money to spend, and she really does need warmer clothes and a haircut.

Plus, shopping with Ramona and Evangeline will definitely be more fun—and more productive—than shopping with Dad.

Still, it won't be the same as shopping with her mother.

I miss you, Mom. I miss you so much.

Aloud, she tells Ramona halfheartedly, "Thanks. That would be fun."

"Good."

Looking at her, Calla has another flash of some inexplicable link to her father.

Come on. Dad and Ramona?

No way, she tells herself again, and heads back toward her grandmother's house.

Strolling to Willow's after one of Odelia's creative stir-fry dinners—this time, a surprisingly good mixture of pork, peanut butter, rice, and bean sprouts—Calla's feeling much better.

She just spoke to her father and mentioned to him that she'll need computer access for a school project.

"Cal, I can't afford to buy—"

"No, Dad, I know," she cut in. "I have an idea, though. What about Mom's laptop?"

He was silent for a minute.

She held her breath, willing him to agree.

"It's back in Florida," he said slowly. "Even if you wanted to—"

"Lisa wants me to visit her. She even sent me an airline voucher. I can go down, and get the computer while I'm there," she pointed out. "You left the keys to the house with the Wilsons."

He didn't argue. He just said he'd think about it, and she left it at that, not wanting to push too hard.

But something tells her she's going to get her hands on her mother's computer files in the near future . . . and that somewhere among them, she might find a clue.

For the time being, though, there's nothing to do but to roll up her sleeves and tackle the math worksheets with Willow. It'll almost be a relief to think about the kind of problems that can actually be solved—and in specific steps, no less. So different from the other kinds of problems she's dealing with lately.

Her father's comment about college last weekend really made her think about next year—about whether she'll be able to get into the schools that topped the list she and her parents had always discussed.

Is that even what she wants, though?

Now that Mom isn't here to motivate her and Dad is a continent away, Calla isn't sure. She does know what Mom would have wanted for her. She'd have been so proud if Calla went to an Ivy League school.

Do I want that? Can I possibly get in?
And can we even afford it if I did?

It doesn't seem likely that she'll be accepted into a top school with a failing math grade, so she'd really better get her butt in gear now. It might already be too late.

As she climbs the steps to Willow's front porch, her train of thought continues to bounce around: Ivy League, Cornell . . .

Kevin. Why did he decide to get in touch out of the blue?

Blue. So he's still interested in her? Is he going to ask her to homecoming? What about Jacy?

Jacy. He was so sweet, bringing her a lunch.

The door opens and her train of thought slams into a brick wall.

An unfamiliar woman is looking out at her. Oops.

"Oh, I'm sorry . . . wrong house." Calla backs away from the door, wondering how she managed to make that mistake. Well, that's what she gets for daydreaming about guys: Kevin, Blue, Jacy.

Wait a minute.

This *is* the right house, she realizes, seeing the street number on the porch pillar.

"Are you looking for Willow?" the stranger asks. "I'm Althea." At Calla's blank look, she clarifies, "Her mother."

What? How is that possible?

The woman in the doorway is the polar opposite of Willow York. Physically, anyway. Her gray hair is short and frizzy, and her face, propped on several chins, is plain. She's morbidly obese, her tremendous arms, legs, and torso crammed into a snug-fitting navy velour sweat suit.

"I . . . um . . . it's nice to, uh, meet you," Calla stammers. She would have expected Willow's mother to be as drop-dead

181

gorgeous as she is—and remembers her earlier assumption that she'd be a doctor or lawyer or banker, like the parents of her schoolmates back in Florida, instead of a medium.

Yeah, just as she originally expected Willow to be snobby and standoffish. Remembering that first day in the cafeteria, when she was surprised to see Willow rescue Donald Reamer and his dropped lunch tray, she feels a stab of guilt.

Come on, Calla. If being in Lily Dale has taught her anything, it's that she should never, ever, EVER subscribe to preconceived notions. Her own or anyone else's.

"It's nice to meet you, too," Althea York is saying. She has kind eyes, Calla notices. And a welcoming smile.

She's sick, though, Calla thinks, and immediately wonders where that odd idea came from. It was a fleeting inspiration, just like the strange flash she had last weekend about her father and Ramona. But this makes less sense than that, even. Why would she get it into her head that a total stranger is sick?

"Come on in. Willow ran to the store for me, but she should be back soon."

"Thank you."

She steps into the front hall and Willow's mother closes the door behind her.

"You can wait for her in the study," she says, and leads the way. Every step she takes is an obvious effort, and she's breathless by the time they reach the kitchen.

Maybe she really is sick. Did Willow mention something about it? Calla doesn't think so, but . . .

"Are you thirsty?" Althea asks. "Can I get you something to—" She breaks off abruptly, her body stiffening and head jerking.

Oh no! Is she having some kind of seizure? What do I do?

"You lost your mother."

It takes Calla a moment to grasp Althea's words and realize there's nothing physically wrong with her. "Oh . . . yes. In July."

Calla is caught off guard, though she probably shouldn't be surprised at this point that yet another stranger knows about Mom's death. Funny how it's almost harder to get used to a small town filled with gossips than a small town filled with spiritualists.

"So, Willow told you?" she asks Althea.

"No, I feel her here."

"What? You feel who here?"

"Your mother. She's with you."

FIFTEEN

"My mother is here?" Calla's knees go liquid and she reaches blindly for something to grab on to, her head spinning.

"Here, sit down." Althea York gently guides her into a chair. "I'm sorry. I didn't mean to upset you."

"No, you didn't . . . I mean . . ." She closes her eyes and tries to focus. There must be a chill, a sense that there's a presence, the scent of lilies of the valley in the room, something she missed . . . and is still missing. Because . . .

"I don't feel her," she tells Willow's mother. "Why don't I feel her?" The question comes out sounding like a pitiful wail, but she can't help it.

"Oh, honey." Althea lowers herself into a chair with a faint groan of effort and takes both Calla's hands in her own. They're sturdy, warm, and reassuring. "Most people aren't aware of Spirit touching in. It's not—"

"No," Calla cuts in, distraught, "that's just it—I *am* aware. I'm . . . like you. And everyone else here."

Althea's eyebrows shoot toward her salt-and-pepper bangs.

"I can see ghosts—I mean, spirits—and hear them and smell them," Calla rushes on, "just like you can. Ever since I got here . . . or maybe before," she adds hurriedly, remembering that first glimpse of Aiyana at the funeral. "It's been happening ever since my mom died. But not *her*. I can't see *her*. And she's the only one who really matters."

Willow's mom is silent for a moment.

Then she says, "I can tell you that this doesn't necessarily work the way—"

Calla bites back a bitter *Here we go again.*

But she's so sick of it.

She's going to tell me it's not like a telephone. That you can't just place a call to someone on the Other Side and expect it to be answered.

"—but," Althea continues, seeing the look on her face, "I have a feeling you've heard that already. Right?"

Calla nods.

"And it doesn't help, does it? When your heart is hurting and you've lost someone you loved, and needed, so desperately, and you'd give anything to have that physical connection one last time . . ."

Has she lost someone, too? Calla wonders, watching her, hearing the note of pain in her voice. *Lost them, and maybe even tried to find them again on the Other Side?*

Or does she just know what it must be like for me?

185

"So, my mother's here?" she asks, looking around the empty room, and Althea nods.

"Can you see her?"

"She looks like you."

Althea's looking at something to Calla's right side and she jerks her head toward the spot, only to find it empty.

"Mom," she whispers, and slips her hand from Althea's to reach into the emptiness, as if she might suddenly be able to touch her mother.

But she doesn't feel her . . . not physically with her hand, not spiritually in the room. She doesn't feel anything at all.

Calla Delaney.

That's her name.

The friendly woman in the café told him, so casually. "Oh, you mean Calla Delaney," she said in response to his question. "Sure, she's Odelia Lauder's granddaughter. Pretty girl, tall, slim, with long, light brown hair—the spitting image of her mother, Stephanie, when she was that age."

"Do you know where Odelia Lauder lives?" was his next question, but by then, the woman's less-cooperative friend had shot her a warning frown, and she promptly claimed that she didn't.

Which was ludicrous, of course, in a town that size. Everyone in Lily Dale knows everyone else—and their business. That's apparent.

All he had to do was stroll down the street and ask the next passerby where Odelia Lauder lived, and he was pointed in the right direction with a cheerful smile.

"There's a sign with her name on it hanging right over her door . . . you can't miss it," he was told.

But when he got here—just a short time ago, under cover of darkness, after killing a few hours in a truck stop off the highway—there was no sign. Just a bracket with a pot of yellow flowers.

So he's been watching the house. Waiting.

He keeps reminding himself that all he wants tonight, before he gets back behind the wheel for the long drive back to Ohio, is a glimpse of her.

But, thoughts racing and body tense from too much truck-stop coffee, he wonders if that can possibly be enough.

"Is it some kind of . . . of block?" Calla asks Althea desperately. "Is that why can't I find my mother? Why can't she come through to me?"

"Oh, honey, you just lost the person who was closest to you in the entire world, and your pain is so overwhelming—so damned huge, pardon my French, and all-encompassing—that it may be acting as a barrier, and you just aren't open to—"

"No, I am! I am open! I swear! My mother is all I think about sometimes. Reaching her . . . I think about it all the time. I look for her everywhere, and—"

"But you're grieving, Calla. You're so young, and you have so much grief to process, such a tremendous amount of healing to do—that burden is more than enough for you to bear. When the time is right, and when you've had some time to heal and fully accept her passing—"

"I *do* accept it," she protests stubbornly.

But it's obvious from Althea's expression that she doesn't agree. Still, she doesn't argue, saying only, "Your loss is so fresh, Calla. When you've had time to process it and get some perspective, I believe your mother will be able to come through to you."

"She will?"

"I believe she will," Althea says carefully.

"Can you ask her for me?"

"Her energy is gone and—"

"You're just saying that to get me off your back," Calla accuses, and is immediately surprised at herself. It isn't like her to talk to anyone this way, let alone an adult—and a virtual stranger.

"No, honey, the energy is really gone." Althea lays a chubby hand on her arm. "But you don't need me to talk to her. You know that, don't you?"

"What do you mean?"

"You can do it yourself. Anytime. You need to realize that."

"It's not the same if I don't know she can hear me," Calla says in a small voice.

"She can."

"But I want to hear her, and see her." And suddenly, she doesn't know how she's going to last until that class on Saturday morning.

"I know you do. But when—if—your mom does come through to you, it might not be in the way you're expecting. Keep in mind that you have to be open to anything."

"There have been a few times . . ." Calla gathers her thoughts, then goes on, "Lilies of the valley were my mother's favorite flower. I've smelled that scent in a couple of places where it shouldn't have been. Do you think that was her?"

"Maybe. Sometimes Spirit makes itself known in unexpected ways. We might receive signs through symbols we don't even recognize because we're so busy looking for whatever it is that we expect."

"But if that's how she makes herself known—through the smell of those flowers—why couldn't I smell it right now?"

"I wish I could answer that for you, Calla, but this isn't an exact science. I can't say that every time you smell lilies of the valley for the rest of your life, it's your mother coming through to you, or that she isn't with you when you don't smell it. Just know that sometimes that may be how she makes herself known to you."

"But she made herself known to you by appearing."

Althea shrugs. "I've been doing this work for years. It's like anything else. You have to work at it."

"I want to see her," Calla repeats stubbornly.

"I know you do. Just remember, physical manifestations aren't the only way our loved ones make themselves known. In fact, sometimes, their visits are so subtle we miss them if we aren't entirely receptive. And sometimes, they even come to us in dreams because we're most open to their energy when we're asleep."

"Dreams?" Calla echoes, her thoughts racing. She thinks about what Dylan said earlier, about seeing the raccoon man in his bed at night. Was that more than just a bad dream? And what about the recurring dream she herself has had about dredging the lake. Is Mom herself sending Calla some kind of message about the long-ago argument with Odelia?

"So if you have a dream," she asks Althea, "how can you tell if—"

A door slams in the front of the house, and Calla clamps her mouth shut. For some reason, she doesn't want Willow to walk in on this particular conversation. It feels too . . . private. Which is kind of ironic, considering she met Althea only about ten minutes ago.

"Here you go, Mom." Willow breezes into the kitchen carrying a white paper bag. "Calla! You're here. Have you been waiting long?"

"No." *Just long enough for a crash course in mediumship.*

"Good. The pharmacist is always slow, but I swear he took forever tonight."

Calla watches Willow hand her mother a receipt and a bag. Medication, obviously. For Althea.

Because she's sick, Calla realizes with a pang of regret. *Really, really sick.*

Again, the thought makes no sense. For all she knows, Althea could be taking antibiotics for a sore throat, but . . .

That's not it.

She feels Althea's serious illness as suddenly and as surely as she's felt other things she couldn't possibly know. Things that turned out to be true.

Watching mother and daughter exchange a smile, she's overwhelmed by a sweeping, inexplicable sadness. She knows with a sickening certainty that Willow York is going to be in Calla's shoes someday. Maybe not long from now.

"So let's get to it." Willow turns to Calla. "Did you bring your stuff?"

"I'll let you girls do your thing." Althea begins moving

with obvious physical effort toward the next room. "I'm glad we met, Calla."

"So am I," she says as casually as she can manage around the aching lump in her throat.

It's late, past nine thirty, when Calla leaves Willow's. Her head is spinning, filled with mathematical formulas and everything Althea told her—and then, of course, there's what happened just now, when she remembered to ask Willow if she could check her e-mail before leaving.

> Calla, It was so good to hear from you. I really miss you and I'm glad you wrote back. Maybe if the weather's nice one of these weekends I'll come visit you in Lily Dale. It's not that long a drive, and any excuse for a road trip in the new car, LOL
>
> Let me know.
>
> xoxo Kevin

She didn't answer it.

Partly because she wasn't sure quite what to make of it. *Any excuse for a road trip?* Is that vaguely insulting? Or just a sign that they're now merely casual, buddy-buddy pals?

And . . . *let me know?* Let him know what? If she wants him to visit?

Does she want him to visit?

The truth is, she longs to see Kevin again . . . but the old Kevin. She wants, more than anything, to go back to the way things were.

Seeing the new Kevin would be just a painful reminder that those days are gone forever . . . wouldn't it?

On the other hand, seeing him—and revisiting the past—might actually help to cure that vague homesickness that pops up every now and then.

Great. So which is it?

As she crosses the quiet street to her grandmother's small patch of front lawn, a familiar, nagging uneasiness creeps over Calla.

Probably just because she's out alone in the dark of night in Lily Dale.

Yeah. And because some little kid said a bad guy is out to get you.

She glances up to see that there's no moon tonight. The sky is black and wisps of mist drift eerily in the yellowish glow above a nearby lamppost.

Pretty spooky. She looks around, half-expecting to find Kaitlyn's spirit hovering nearby, but it isn't.

Still, she has the distinct feeling that she's not alone out here. That someone is watching her.

Which is crazy.

Are you really going to let a five-year-old put crazy ideas into your head?

Heart pounding, she hurriedly climbs Odelia's front steps, noticing she has yet to rehang the shingle with her name on it.

Calla opens the door. Of course it's unlocked, as always, and of course she finds herself thinking, as always, that her grandmother shouldn't be quite so reckless.

She slides the bolt behind her, and for the first time, doesn't feel entirely secure even then.

Through the window in the door, Calla looks out into the night. The glare from the porch light makes it impossible to see beyond, and she wonders if someone really is lurking out there, in the inky shadows.

Someone dead? Or someone alive?

Thinking of Kaitlyn, and Erin, she shudders and turns away. *Stop freaking yourself out. You're being ridiculous.*

The sound of the television from the next room is a normal and welcome distraction, and she takes a few deep breaths to calm herself.

Okay. Good. Everything is fine. See?

In the living room, she finds Odelia snoozing in her chair in front of a *CSI* rerun.

Calla hesitates for a moment, wondering if she should wake her to say she's home.

Or . . .

You can quietly go make a phone call without being overheard.

Opting for plan B, she tiptoes past her grandmother into the kitchen, which is bathed in a cozy glow from the bulb beneath the stove hood. As Calla reaches for the phone, something darts across the room.

That was her, Calla, suddenly appearing out of the darkness and disappearing into the house just now.

He knows, without a doubt, that it had to be her.

She looks just like the woman's description.

And she's beautiful, like the others.

Beautiful, and afraid . . . yes, like the others.

But he found them, their pictures, by chance. Followed

them, learned their routines, waiting oh so patiently to strike. And they fell for his ploy, believing, at least at first, that he was a police officer trying to help them. It was almost surprising, how easy it was to lure them in.

Then again, those girls didn't have some kind of crazy sixth sense. They weren't the least bit suspicious of him.

This girl might be different.

He was so startled to see her out here, alone in the dark, that he simply froze.

You missed your chance. There she was, a few feet away, all alone on a deserted street. He could simply have reached out and—

Yes, but it isn't time.

He's known all along that he isn't going to do anything tonight, no matter how badly his hands ache to grab her.

He clenches them into fists, fighting the urge, knowing he can't rush into anything on the spur of the moment.

These things take time. He has to be in the right frame of mind. He has to have a plan. He has to be ready to cover his tracks.

For now, he should be content to just watch her, to savor each moment, knowing that he alone controls her fate.

"Gert! Geez, you scared the heck out of me!" Calla plucks the kitten from the kitchen floor and holds her close, stroking two fingertips over the soft fur between the delicate little ears. "I'm such a nervous wreck tonight. What's up with me?"

Gert rewards her petting with a purr that is surprisingly

strong for a creature her size, and Calla smiles as she dials the phone.

What an adorable kitten, she thinks.

Which leads illogically to, *What if Kevin and Annie broke up?*

Seriously. What if he came to his senses and realized he and Calla belong together and is trying to feel her out, wondering if she'd be open to hooking up again?

She can't keep wondering. She has to find out, so that she can either move on, once and for all, or . . .

Or what?

Get back together with Kevin?

She tells herself that would be a terrible idea. For plenty of reasons.

She just can't seem to think of any off the top of her head.

The phone is already ringing on the other end of the line.

"Hello?"

"Lisa! It's me."

"Tiffany?"

Stung, she replies, "No . . . Calla." Tiffany Foxwood goes to Shoreside Day School with Lisa—and isn't one of Calla's favorite people in the world.

"Calla! Wow, it's so good to hear your voice!"

Wondering if Lisa and Tiffany have been hanging out, she tries to say lightly, "That's funny, since you didn't even recognize it."

It comes out entirely the wrong way, though, and Lisa snaps back in her familiar drawl, "Well, it's been a while since I've heard it. How come you never called me back the other day?"

"I'm sorry," Calla says immediately, and means it. "I know I've been bad about staying in touch since you left. It's just . . . I've had a lot going on."

"I know what you mean. It's been crazy here, too, between school and cheerleading practice and trying to find something to wear for senior portrait day."

Knowing Lisa can't possibly understand that what Calla's been through this last week in Lily Dale can't begin to compare to her own life, she asks, "What's been going on at school? Fill me in."

As Lisa talks about people she used to know and places she used to go, Calla finds herself wistful, once again, for the routine daily life she left behind in Florida. She never realized, at the time, just how blessed she really was. It isn't only about having lost Mom—or even Kevin.

It's just . . .

Having exchanged ordinary for extraordinary, she wonders if she'll ever get used to seeing and hearing what others can't, to disembodied shadows and spirits popping up to show her bloody corpses, to just knowing things about other people, strangers, even—things she can't possibly know.

"I'm going on and on," Lisa says after a few minutes of updating Calla, "and you haven't even told me how you like your new school."

"Oh . . . it's good."

"Have you made some new friends besides . . . what's the name of that girl next door?"

"Evangeline. Yeah, I've made a few. This girl, Willow—I eat lunch with her and another girl, Sarita. They're really nice." Before Calla left tonight, Willow said something about sitting together in the cafeteria again tomorrow, so Pam—or Shakespeare—at lunch is history, thank goodness.

"What about those guys?" Lisa asks. "Blue and Jason?"

"Jacy." Wow. It seems like a million years ago that Calla told her about them, but it was only a few weeks, right on the heels of finding out about Annie, so she made it sound as though she were juggling two guys.

"Did you choose?" Lisa asks. "Or are you still into both of them?"

"Oh, uh, I'm going out with Blue Saturday night, and . . . and I had lunch with Jacy the other day. So, yeah. Both, I guess."

"Lucky you." Lisa fills her in on her own love life. She's decided she has a crush on Nick Rodriguez, but he's going out with Brittany Jensen, though he keeps flirting with Lisa when Brittany's not around.

"What do you think I should do about Nick?" Lisa asks.

"I don't think you should do anything right now," she says firmly. "Let him make a move, if he's going to."

"I guess you're right. I just don't think he's really all that into Brittany."

The conversation drifts on, and Calla lets Lisa do most of the talking.

"It's so hard to do all this catching up in one quick phone call," Lisa says. "When are you coming to visit? You got the airline voucher, right?"

"I got it. I'm not sure. My dad doesn't want me to leave here just yet," she white-lies.

"I wish you were at least online, so we could stay in touch better. And you could blog again, and update your MySpace page. People have been asking what's up with you."

Calla murmurs an agreement, but she can't help thinking it would feel wrong to go back to blogging these days. She can't imagine sharing most of the details of her daily life with anyone in her old world, let alone putting it out there in cyberspace.

"When I do eventually get down there, I'm going to get my mom's old laptop and use that here," she tells Lisa. "My dad said it would be okay."

"That would be great! The sooner the better, right?"

"Right." *I guess.*

"You name the weekend, and I'll start making plans," Lisa tells her, and Calla halfheartedly promises to do just that. It won't be for a while, though. As much as she misses Lisa—and as much as she wants a computer to use—she isn't particularly eager to face her old house and its bloody memories.

Realizing she should probably hang up and get busy on the rest of her homework, she says, "Listen, I just wanted to ask you one last thing . . . about Kevin. How's he doing?"

"He's good. Actually, that's funny, because I just talked to him, and he asked me about you, too."

"What did he ask?"

"Just what you were up to lately. I think he misses you . . . although when I asked him if he was going to break up with Annie, he got annoyed."

"They're still together?"

"Yeah."

"Why'd you ask him about breaking up with her? I thought you liked her?"

"I do. But I love you. Anyway, Kevin's talking about bringing Annie down here for Thanksgiving, so . . ."

So, so much for that, Calla thinks.

She hangs up with Lisa a few minutes later, with a promise to call and e-mail more regularly, and a "love you, too," in response to Lisa's.

Wiping her wet eyes, she realizes that lately, her life is all about missing people. Lisa, her father, her mother, Kevin.

Yeah. But no way is Calla going to tell Kevin to come visit her in Lily Dale.

Why should she?

He has Annie, she reminds herself as she turns off the kitchen lights and heads into the living room. *And you have enough friends.*

No, she doesn't need one more. Especially not one who shattered her heart and wasn't there when she needed him most.

Calla's thoughts drift back to Althea York and what happened in her kitchen. So, Mom's spirit really is around her. Somehow, that's almost more frustrating than it was thinking her mother had simply ceased to exist.

Mom's still out there . . . or right here. I just have to get past this block and open myself to her.

Back in the living room, she gently touches her grandmother's shoulder.

"What? What?" Odelia wakes with a start.

"I'm home, Gammy, and it's getting late. Come up to bed."

"Oh . . . I'll be up in a minute. Did you lock up?"

"Mmm-hmm."

"Are you sure?" Odelia sits up straighter in her chair and looks at Calla, once again triggering that sense of uneasiness.

Why is she asking about locking the door? She never has before.

"I'll double-check," she tells her grandmother, frowning, thinking about Dylan and his dream and wondering if Odelia is worried for any particular reason.

Calla goes into the front hall, where she finds that the door is, indeed, locked. She turns the switch by the door and the outdoor light goes off.

Almost immediately, she realizes that someone is standing beside a tree just across the way.

Shocked, Calla feels her breath lodge in her throat as she gapes at the silhouette of a human figure wearing a long dark coat or cloak.

Goose bumps sting the back of Calla's neck as she watches whoever—whatever—it is slip away into the shadows, leaving her to wonder if her imagination is playing tricks on her . . . or if someone really is out there.

Is it Spirit?

Or is it human?

It's no one, she tells herself firmly. *You're losing it. You really are.*

Exhausted—physically and emotionally—she forces herself to turn away, to climb the stairs, to sit at her desk and tackle her homework.

After she finally gives up and climbs into bed, though, it takes a long time for her to drift off to sleep.

When she does, she dreams that she's being chased by a menacing figure in black, and she can hear her mother somewhere in the distance, frantically screaming at her to run for her life.

Did she see him when she turned off the light and looked out the window of her grandmother's house?

Or did she just feel his presence, the way people like her claim to do?

You think you know everything, he taunts her silently as he drives back down the thruway toward Ohio.

Well then, you must know I'm coming to get you.

And you must be afraid.

His lips curl into a smile. All the better.

Now that he's seen her, it doesn't even matter that she doesn't have long blond hair. No, it doesn't matter at all. Because killing her, and putting an end to her meddling, will be more satisfying than what he's done to any of the others or what he's going to do to Hayley Gorzynski when her turn comes. And again and again, after that.

But Calla Delaney will come first.

Sweet dreams, Calla. Until we meet again . . .

SIXTEEN

Thursday, September 13
7:27 p.m.

As dusk falls over Lily Dale the following night, Calla finds herself standing beneath another medium's shingle at yet another unfamiliar Lily Dale cottage.

This one is neatly kept and fairly modern, located at the far eastern end of town, on Erie Boulevard—a narrow, rutted road that is like no other boulevard Calla has ever known.

"Are you positive we should be doing this?" Calla asks Jacy as she peers through the slatted screened window of the metal front door.

The glassed-in porch looks like an extension of the house, with teal carpet, several lamps, a television, a dining set, and lots of white indoor-outdoor furniture topped in bright blue-and-white striped vinyl cushions.

"No. I'm not *positive.*" Jacy's finger is poised over the bell as he turns to look at her. "But what other option is there?"

Oh, geez. Why did he sound so much more convincing earlier, at school? When she told him she was ready to confront Darrin's parents, he said he was glad she had decided to go ahead with it, that he would go with her, and that they shouldn't waste any time because the Yateses usually head out to Arizona for the winter.

"You're not very reassuring, Jacy," Calla hisses now. "We should leave."

All at once, a dog erupts in frantic barking from somewhere inside.

"I think it's too late for that," Jacy says, a moment before the door leading from the house to the closed-in porch is thrown open.

The man on the threshold is mostly bald, with a fringe of gray hair and wire-framed bifocals. He's wearing a dark green cardigan sweater and corduroy slippers. There's a folded newspaper in his hand. At a glance, he could be anyone's grandfather.

I'm glad he's not mine, though, Calla can't help thinking. He would have been, if Mom had stayed with his son Darrin instead of moving on and meeting Dad.

Then again, if that had happened, she would never have been born in the first place.

The thought makes her shudder inwardly as Mr. Yates steps into the porch, peering out at them through the slatted window of the outer door. "Yes? Did you want a reading?"

"No!" Calla replies quickly. "I just wanted to ask you about something."

He opens the door a crack. "Pardon me?"

"Bob? Who is it?" calls a female voice inside the house. Calla can hear jangling dog tags and paws tapping on the floor, and the woman says faintly, "Be still, Jasmine."

"I'm sorry . . . how can I help you?" Mr. Yates asks Calla, looking more closely at her. "Have we met? You look familiar."

"No, we haven't met." *But some people say I look just like my mother.*

My dead mother.

Whom your son might have—

"She's new here," Jacy cuts into her grim thoughts.

The man's faded gray-blue eyes flick in his direction. "You, I recognize," he tells Jacy. "You're the boy who's living with Walt and Peter, right?"

"Right." Jacy nods.

"Mr. Yates," Calla speaks up as footsteps sound in the house behind him, "I wanted to ask about your son Darrin."

She hears a gasp and realizes a woman—Darrin's mother; she has to be—has appeared behind Mr. Yates.

"Bob!" the woman says sharply. She's wiry and short, with cropped silver hair and angular features. "Who are these kids?"

"I . . . I'm not quite sure." The old man levels a thoughtful gaze at Calla. "Why are you asking about my son?"

"Because . . ." She takes a deep breath and prepares to deliver her bombshell. "I think I saw him."

She waits for the inevitable shocked reaction.

For some reason, it doesn't come.

Mr. Yates merely blinks behind his thick glasses. Mrs. Yates presses her hands to her forehead. Her bony fingers remind Calla of a bird's claws.

"Where did you see him?"

"In . . . Florida," Calla replies to Mr. Yates, realizing he and his wife must have already known their son is out there somewhere, and not . . . dead.

Like Mom, she thinks bitterly, and clenches her fists in her jacket pockets.

"Well, that's a first, huh, Betty?" Mr. Yates asks with a tight-lipped smile. "Florida."

His wife doesn't reply, just shakes her head wearily.

"So, you know Darrin's alive?" Jacy asks.

"If he isn't, I'd be surprised," Mrs. Yates says. "Bob and I have consulted enough of our colleagues over the years who told us they feel that he's still on the earth plane."

"What about you?" Calla asks. "You're mediums yourselves. Couldn't you figure that out on your own?"

She remembers, then, something Ramona told her soon after she arrived in Lily Dale, when she asked how Darrin's parents, as psychic mediums, could possibly not know what happened to their son.

"Nothing is more powerful than the bond between a parent and a child," Ramona replied. "There are some things a parent might not want to see, or accept."

Yes. And the same thing might be true with a child, Calla admits to herself, remembering what Althea said about her own grief acting as a barrier to her mother on the Other Side.

Neither of the Yateses chooses to answer Calla's question now.

Instead, Mr. Yates asks one of his own. "When did you see Darrin in Florida?"

"In March. And again in July, at my mother's . . . funeral."

She stares—or maybe it's more like glares—from Mr. Yates to Mrs. Yates. "I think he might have had something to do with her death."

Jacy elbows her.

She ignores him. "Darrin was my mother's boyfriend years ago, before he disappeared from Lily Dale. And now I'm getting all kinds of signs that seem to be linking him to what happened to her, and—"

"What is your mother's name?" Betty Yates interrupts, her voice and expression much chillier than they were moments ago.

"It's—I mean it *was*—Stephanie Delaney. Stephanie Lauder."

The Yateses look at each other.

Then, as if in unspoken agreement with his wife, Bob Yates says, "I need to ask you to leave."

Jacy begins, "Sir, I'm so sorry—we're so sorry—and we didn't mean to—"

"Go."

"But my mother—"

"I'm sorry about your mother," Betty says stiffly, "but my son had nothing to do with whatever it was that happened to her."

"How can you know that if you don't even know where—"

"Darrin would never have hurt Stephanie. He loved her more than anyone else on earth." *Including me.*

The last two words are unspoken, but they seem to hang in the air as if Darrin's mother had actually spoken them.

"God only knows what Stephanie said or did to make our son decide to disappear," Mrs. Yates goes on, "but—"

"So, you blame my mother for your son's problems?" Calla cuts in incredulously. "Why?"

"Go," Mr. Yates says again, more wearily. "Please. Just go."

"But I—"

Calla's protest is cut off by the door being closed in her face. Jaw hanging, she looks at Jacy.

"Come on," he says quietly.

They walk in silence for a few blocks.

After they've turned the corner, away from the boulevard, Calla stops walking and looks at Jacy.

"I can't just drop this."

"No. I know."

She wishes she could see his face, but it's cast in shadows. "So what do I do now?"

"I don't think we're going to get anywhere with them. And there's something . . ." Jacy shakes his head. "I don't know. I'm worried."

"About them?"

"No. About . . . ," he trails off.

"About me?" Calla asks, and he nods.

Immediately, her heart picks up a little. Out of fear, because of Dylan's warning and now Jacy's . . . and, maybe, just a little, because Jacy cares enough about her to worry about her.

"Why?" she asks, trying to sound far more casual than she feels.

"I don't know. Just be careful, okay?"

"Okay." She pauses. "I'm going to a class with Evangeline

over the weekend. Beginning mediumship. I thought that might help."

"That's good. Really good."

"Have you taken any classes?"

"No. Not because I don't think they're worth it, but just because . . . I don't know. Classes aren't my thing."

Yeah. She can sense that, whenever she sees him in school. He always has a restless air about him. He's much more relaxed when he's outside. Like now.

They start walking again.

"Do you believe what they said?" she asks after a while. "That my mom's the one who did something to make Darrin disappear? Because Ramona said he was on drugs. Maybe they didn't know about that."

"Maybe not."

"Maybe I should tell them."

"Their son is missing. Their hearts are broken. They aren't going to be very open to some stranger who shows up and basically accuses him of being a druggie and a murderer."

"I know. And I'm sorry I said that to them." Calla sighs. "I know I got carried away. I just . . . I couldn't help it."

To her shock, Jacy reaches over and takes her hand. Giving it a squeeze, he says, "I know how brutal this has to be for you."

She nods, not daring to speak . . . or even breathe.

He doesn't drop her hand.

They walk on in silence.

Holding hands.

As overwhelmed as Calla is by everything else that's happened, right here, right now, Jacy Bly is all she can think about.

Her hand feels so safe in his warm, protective grasp. She

wishes there was a longer way home, but all too soon, they've reached Odelia's house.

Jacy walks her up onto the front porch, and she wishes the stupid porch light weren't on, because she has a feeling he wants to kiss her goodnight and she seriously doubts he's going to do it in a spotlight.

Kiss you goodnight? What are you, crazy? He's not going to—
Or is he?

A glimmer in his black eyes makes her pulse race as, still holding her hand, he says, "Calla."

Then she hears it.

The squeak of the Taggarts' front door, a stone's throw away.

Evangeline. No!

Calla wrenches her hand from Jacy's just in time to see Mason Taggart step out onto the porch across the way. He doesn't even glance in their direction as he retrieves something from a chair and goes back inside, banging the door behind him.

But it's too late to reclaim the moment.

Hands shoved deep in his pockets, Jacy is already turning away. Sounding shy, or maybe hurt, he says, "See you tomorrow, then."

"Jacy."

"Yeah?"

Come back.

Please.

Kiss me goodnight.

But, of course, Calla doesn't say any of those things.

She says only, "Thanks for going with me."

"Yeah. No problem," he replies, and is swallowed by the darkness.

Calla turns toward the door, then stops short.

There, on the clapboard wall beside it, are a pair of shadows. Her own, and a disembodied one beside it.

It's nearly identical in size, a clearly human form although the outline isn't as sharply defined as Calla's own silhouette.

She turns, knowing before she sees it that the spot beside her will be empty.

Someone is here beside her, though. Maybe that's all she's supposed to know. But is that enough? Can it ever be enough?

She watches the shadow until it fades away.

Then she goes into the house, alone once more.

SEVENTEEN

Saturday, September 15
10:10 a.m.

On Saturday morning, Calla is prepared to tell her grandmother she and Evangeline are going out for a walk. Luckily, Odelia is behind closed doors with a client when she comes downstairs for breakfast, so the cover story isn't necessary. It wouldn't have been believable on a day like this. A cold rain is falling as Calla steps out onto the porch.

She looks up at the sky and finds it in motion as endless masses of purple-gray clouds shift across.

Should she go back for an umbrella? It doesn't look like this is going to let up anytime soon.

"I've got one," Evangline's voice calls, and she looks up to see her friend descending the steps next door, beneath a huge black umbrella.

"How'd you know what I was thinking?" Calla asks with a grin as she splashes down the path to join her.

"I saw you look up at the sky, and I noticed you didn't have an umbrella. What else would you be thinking? Not that I'm not psychic," Evangeline adds cheerfully. "Just . . . you don't have to be, to figure out some things."

No. But you might have to be, to figure out others. Like why she'd have dreamed, last night, about Olivia Newton John. The details were fuzzy when she woke up, but Calla knows she was wearing a 1950s-style ponytail and letterman's sweater. Like she did in the movie *Grease*.

As they make their way up Library Street toward the mediums' league building, she tells Evangeline about it, and about the disembodied voice singing "Hopelessly Devoted to You" in the school auditorium the other day.

"What do you think it all means?" Calla asks.

"I have no idea."

"Okay, then, what about this? I've seen human silhouettes a few times on the wall next to mine . . . and there's no one there beside me where someone would have to be standing."

"Shadow ghosts." Evangeline nods.

"You've heard of them?"

"Yeah, but I've never seen one. Sometimes they're supposed to just look like mist or a cloud darting around, but sometimes they're actual human shadows. Kind of creepy."

"Ye-ah!" Calla says in a no-kidding tone. "Especially when you're totally alone, at night. So are they just . . . regular ghosts?"

Evangeline hesitates. "I don't know much about that."

Yes, you do, Calla thinks. *You just don't want to tell me. Why not?*

"Maybe you should ask Patsy," Evangeline adds quickly, as

if sensing Calla is about to press her on it. "She's the teacher for this class we're going to."

"Patsy Metcalf, registered medium and spiritual consultant?" Calla recites.

"You already know her?"

"Just her sign."

"Well, I promise you'll love her."

A minute later, they step into the building. As Evangeline collapses the umbrella just inside the door, Calla looks around.

The old-fashioned structure seems to consist of one circular room with what appears to be a small kitchen and bathroom off the back. The color scheme is a soothing blue and white, with farmhouse-style beadboard halfway up the wall. There are tall windows all the way around, topped with stained-glass panels in shades of blue.

In the center, a ring of folding chairs is clustered around a lit candle. A few people—a college-aged man with a beard, a pair of older women, and another girl—are already sitting in them, chatting quietly. Calla recognizes the girl: it's Lena, whose locker is near hers at school.

Their eyes meet, and Lena gives her a welcoming, but obviously surprised, smile.

"Where do you want to sit?" Evangeline asks, leading the way toward the circle of chairs.

"I'll just sit over there on the sidelines and watch." Calla feels self-conscious and is beginning to wish she hadn't come.

"You can't do that. We need your energy here in the circle."

She frowns, wondering if Evangeline is just making that up to convince her.

Before she can respond, the door opens and a petite middle-aged woman blows in with a gust of damp chill.

"Yuck!" she exclaims, shaking her short brown hair like a wet dog. "It's miserable out there this morning! Hi, everyone."

"Come on," Evangeline says, dragging Calla toward the teacher. "I'll introduce you."

"I don't know . . . I think I should just go," she murmurs, but it's too late.

"Patsy, this is my friend Calla," Evangeline announces. "She's sitting in on the class today, remember?"

"I do. You're Odelia's granddaughter, right?"

"Right." No secrets in this town. Calla is glad she didn't lie to her grandmother about where she was going this morning. She'd probably have found out anyway.

Why not just tell her in the first place? she asks herself as Patsy instructs her and Evangeline to sit in the two chairs to her immediate right.

Because this is complicated, that's why. It's not like you're taking piano lessons or something.

No, her being here is wrapped up in Mom and Kaitlyn and Erin, and Calla doesn't feel like sharing any of that with her grandmother just yet.

Now, though, it looks like she'll have to. She wonders how long it'll take for word of her being here to get back to Odelia.

As other students arrive and fill the circle, Patsy goes around the room, handing out today's lesson plan, which centers around something called thought forms.

After everyone holds hands for a brief prayer—new to Calla, whose family never even went to church—Patsy goes through the lesson plan step-by-step. As she discusses techniques mediums use to tune in to people's—and spirits'—thought vibrations, Calla finds herself captivated.

"As mediums, we place ourselves in a subjective state through meditation," Patsy informs the class. "It's like anything else. Just about anyone can do this, to some degree—though some are born with a particular talent and an inherent heightened sense of awareness."

Calla remembers what Evangeline told her, that Calla herself was born with a caul.

She'd love to ask Patsy about that, but she's too shy to raise her hand. Maybe later. Or some other time.

If you decide to come back.

"Our skills improve with practice," Patsy goes on, "just like an athlete's, or an artist's, for example. We can learn to flex our psychic muscles in order to receive the energy that makes up thought vibrations, and to interpret it."

She goes on to say that a body is simply a house for the soul to inhabit while on the earth plane. When the physical body dies, the brain dies with it. But not the mind. The mind is a part of the soul, and that is immortal.

Thinking of her mother, Calla is comforted by that . . . but only to a certain extent.

I really do believe you're still alive, Mom, on some other plane. But I wish you were still on this one, with me.

All too soon, the class has drawn to an end.

"Next week, we'll be doing a hands-on exercise called reading billets," Patsy announces after the closing prayer. "It's something spiritualists used to do in order to prove their abilities to skeptics. Calla, will you be with us again?"

"I'm . . . not sure. Maybe."

"Well, you're more than welcome to join the class," Patsy says so easily that Calla is seized by an impulse to pull her aside and ask her about the *Grease* dream and shadow ghosts and cauls, among other things.

But now isn't the time. There's already a mini-lineup of students clustered nearby, all waiting for their chance to talk to the instructor.

"Do you want to wait?" Evangeline asks as she and Calla pull on their jackets.

"No, that's okay. Maybe I'll come back next week."

"You should. Talk to Odelia about it. I'm sure she'll want you to do this, if you talk to her."

"I know, it's just . . . I've got so much going on today. Maybe later."

"Oh—you're going out with Blue tonight!" Evangeline remembers. As if that's all Calla's got on her mind. "Did you figure out what you're going to wear yet?"

"Not yet. Want to come over and help me decide?"

"Definitely. I bet he asks you to homecoming tonight."

"I wouldn't hold my breath," Calla tells her.

An odd sense of expectation has hung over Calla all afternoon.

She's got an inexplicable, growing feeling something's going to happen tonight.

She just wishes she could be certain it's going to be something pleasant.

The vague, nagging anxiety seems to grow more and more

pronounced as she puts on makeup, fixes her hair, and gets dressed up in a cute blue skirt and top she and Evangeline settled on earlier.

She keeps assuring herself that it's just normal predate nerves, not some kind of warning about impending danger. After all, it's not like Aiyana has popped up lately.

Still . . .

"Make sure you lock the door and take your key with you tonight," Odelia says when she sticks her head into Calla's room to say she's leaving for her Saturday night circle.

Calla feels another twinge of uneasiness.

"Why are we locking the door all of a sudden, Gammy?"

Her grandmother just shrugs.

Did Odelia have some kind of premonition? Did Dylan?

And what about Jacy? He said when they were walking home from the Yateses' that he's worried about her.

Right . . . she almost forgot about that.

She sits on the edge of the bed and puts on a pair of gold earrings, feeling her grandmother's eyes on her.

"You look beautiful," Odelia says with approval as Gert purrs and rubs herself against Calla's ankles.

"Thanks, Gammy."

"I hope you have a good time. What time do you think you'll be home?"

Mom would have told me exactly when to be home, and warned me not to be late, Calla thinks with a pang of grief-tainted irony.

"I'm not sure. Late, I guess. He said we'd get something to eat after the concert."

"I probably won't be back until after midnight myself. Just be careful."

"I will." Calla smiles at her grandmother, wishing she didn't look so . . . worried.

Maybe it's because Calla's driving all the way to Buffalo with Blue in his fancy BMW. Or maybe because she doesn't approve of Blue's father's high-profile lifestyle.

Yeah, or maybe she thinks a raccoon-eyed killer is going to come after me.

Left alone with the kitten in the empty house, Calla realizes she still has fifteen minutes before Blue picks her up. She spends a few minutes pacing around, jumping at every slight creak, before realizing this is silly. She should just wait outside.

"Sorry," she tells Gert as she steps out onto the porch, using her foot to gently keep the kitten inside as she pulls the door shut. She locks it, then turns the handle to try it.

Gert shoots her an accusing look through the glass, then trots back toward the kitchen.

The rain has stopped, leaving Lily Dale glistening and misty as twilight falls.

Sitting on the porch, Calla wishes the Taggarts would show up on theirs, but the house is dark and the driveway empty. Evangeline said Ramona was taking her and Mason out to eat tonight.

Spotting a figure sprinting down Cottage Row toward her, she realizes it's Jacy. He's wearing gray sweats and sneakers, obviously taking his nightly run.

She doesn't know whether to call out to him or hope he doesn't spot her. She hasn't seen him since he left her at the door after almost kissing her . . . or so it seemed.

Watching him look up toward Odelia's house, she realizes

he almost seems to be looking for . . . something? Someone? Her?

When he sees her, he hesitates only briefly before waving. She watches as he slows his pace and jogs toward her.

"How's it going?" he calls from the street.

"Good."

"Good."

She sees his dark eyes checking her out from head to toe. Is he going to ask her why she's all dressed up? Ask her where she's going? And with whom?

Nope.

Maybe he already knows, she realizes. Just like everyone around here seems to know everything.

"Got to keep my heart rate up," he announces. "So, see ya."

"See ya," she calls back, disappointed, and watches him literally run away from her.

That's just because he's training for track, she tells herself.

But she isn't so sure.

So far, Calla's date with Blue has been as close to perfect as any date she's ever had. Including with Kevin.

No, Blue isn't Kevin. And she isn't in love with him.

He isn't Jacy, either.

But Blue is fun and funny and cool—not to mention hot. Plus, he's so at ease in any situation that Calla finds herself instinctively relaxing whenever she's around him.

At the concert—where they had great seats, comp tickets someone gave to Blue's dad—Calla discovered she really likes jazz, and told him so. Afterward, he asked her if she likes wings, too.

"You mean Buffalo wings?" she asked, hoping "wings" isn't some style of music she never heard of. She gets the impression that well-traveled, worldly, wealthy Blue is far more sophisticated than she could ever hope to be.

He laughed. But not because she was ignorant about music. No, just about chicken, apparently.

"We don't call them that around here," he said with a grin.

"What?"

"Buffalo wings. That's a dead giveaway that you're a tourist. In western New York, they're just wings. And you've never had them until you've had them at the Anchor Bar. Those are the real deal."

The Anchor Bar turned out to be a jam-packed, no-frills restaurant right downtown, not far from the concert hall. And Blue was right. She's never had wings like this.

Sitting at a cozy table in the big, brick-walled dining room, they polished off a gigantic bucketful of wings so hot they're listed on the menu as "suicidal," and a pitcher of Pepsi to cool the flames. They also split a sandwich, another local delicacy, called "beef on weck."

Calla was stuffed by the time it arrived, but Blue made her taste it. She bit into a heap of thinly sliced rare roast beef, served with au jus and horseradish on a "kimmelweck"—a big roll sprinkled with crunchy pretzel salt and caraway seeds.

It was awesome.

The whole date was awesome.

How can anything bad happen now?

It can't, Calla decides, riding home beside Blue in the darkness of his car, with an old John Mayer song playing on the radio. It just can't.

She wonders what to do when they reach her grandmother's house.

Odelia won't be home yet.

Back when Calla was dating Kevin, an empty house meant a rare opportunity to be alone together.

But Blue isn't Kevin, and this is barely their third date.

Still . . . he's incredibly good-looking, and she's just as attracted to him—tonight, anyway—as she ever was to Kevin.

Which is exactly why you shouldn't be alone with him, she tells herself firmly.

Okay. So she won't ask him to come in when they get to Odelia's.

She'll just kiss him goodnight here in the car, and that will be that.

Ha. Easier said than done.

Because when Blue pulls up in front of the house, he immediately cuts the engine. "Looks like nobody's home, huh?"

Calla looks up to see that the porch light is on and there's a lamp lit inside. "How can you tell?"

"Your grandmother's car is gone."

"Oh, right. She went, uh, to . . ." She can't even remember at the moment, because Blue is leaning toward her and pulling her close.

"Hmm?" he asks as he wraps his arms around her.

"Uh—"

He cuts off anything she might have said—not that it was

likely to have made much sense—with a kiss. Not just a peck goodnight. A full-fledged, sweeping, passionate, expert kiss that leaves Calla feeling absolutely light-headed. And terrified.

Whoa. This must be why I felt like I was in some kind of danger all day.

She's playing with fire here—and having been once burned by her old flame, she'd be smart to douse this new flame. For now, anyway.

"Can I come in with you, Calla?"

"Yes," she says weakly, then, getting hold of herself, "I mean, no. No!"

"No?" He seems taken aback.

"My grandmother doesn't want me to have anyone in the house when she's not home."

"Odelia said that?" he sounds doubtful.

Yeah, well, he knows her grandmother. Everyone in Lily Dale knows her grandmother, who sticks an expired parking ticket on her own windshield to keep the traffic cops away whenever she parks illegally. She's not exactly a stickler for rules—following anyone else's or imposing her own.

Still . . .

"She's way more strict with me than you'd think," Calla tells Blue in a rush. "She said no one's even allowed on the porch when she's not home, so . . . I'll just say goodnight here."

"Wait, Calla—"

"Goodnight!" she says brightly, and springs from the car, then leans back in to say politely, "Thanks so much for everything."

"Wait one second, will you?" He grabs her hand.

"I have to—"

"Can I just ask you one question?"

"What is it?" she asks, slightly breathless and wondering if she can stick to her guns if he asks her again if he can come in.

But he doesn't. He asks, "Want to go to the homecoming dance with me?"

She gasps. "Yes!"

"Great."

Blue grins.

Calla grins back. Then she remembers something. "What about Willow?"

"What about her?"

"I thought you were . . . you know. Talking to her about homecoming."

"About being on the committee? Yeah. She won't leave me alone about that, but I keep telling her, I'm too busy with other stuff."

So that was it. Blue was e-mailing Willow about the homecoming dance *committee*, not about going to the dance itself. That was all.

"Are you sure I can't come in even for a few minutes?" he asks Calla, and she jolts back to the present.

"Oh—uh, yeah, I'm sure. Sorry. Goodnight!" With that, she practically flies up the path, onto the porch. Turning back toward the car, she gives Blue one last wave.

He blinks the headlights at her and the engine roars to life.

Calla reaches for the knob before remembering that her grandmother said the door would be locked tonight.

Again, she wonders if Odelia had some kind of premonition about something happening to her.

She turns abruptly back toward Blue's car, suddenly not

anxious to be alone in the house, even if it means being alone with Blue. Too late. He's already pulling away.

Okay.

No big deal.

You've been alone before in this house at night. Right? Right.

She unlocks the door, closes it behind her, and locks it again securely.

There. Better already, she tells herself. *Right?*

Wrong.

Her heart is pounding as she walks through the quiet house, hoping the kitten doesn't jump out at her again to-night. Her nerves can't handle that.

"Gert?" she calls, and notices her voice warbles a little. *Oh, please. You're such a chicken. Get a grip, will you?*

She turns on the light as she passes through the dining room toward the kitchen.

"Where are you, kitty?"

No meow or scampering paws in response.

Okay, that's strange.

In the few short days Gert's been here, the kitten has learned to come running when Calla calls.

"Gert!" she calls, more forcefully this time.

In response, she hears a faint meow from the back of the house.

Creeping into the kitchen, she sees that the door to Odelia's sunroom is closed.

"Gert?"

Again, she hears the kitten mew—this time, obviously from behind the door.

How did she get in there?

Maybe Odelia came back home at some point after Calla left and put her in there.

But why would she do that?

Who knows? Maybe because the cat got into something.

Then again, yesterday Gert knocked over a vase of cut flowers, breaking the vase and showering the carpet with water and broken stems, and Odelia barely batted an eye. "Cats will be cats," she said with a shrug.

Okay, so even if she's not worried about the kitten wrecking the house, maybe she was worried that Gert would hurt herself by getting into something dangerous.

Dangerous.

Calla walks stealthily toward the door, growing more uneasy with every step.

Aside from the wedge of light falling across the linoleum through the doorway of the dining room, the kitchen is dark. Even the light under the stove hood, which Odelia usually leaves on, is turned off tonight.

Wait a minute.

In that corner, by the sink . . . there seems to be a faint glow coming from somewhere, Calla realizes. Her eye goes to the window above the sink, but the curtains are drawn.

Somehow, though, a pool of light reflected from . . . somewhere . . . is falling over the pile of clean dishes Odelia left to dry.

Seeing something glint, Calla steps closer, frowning.

The light is beaming off the blade of the knife her grandmother used to make the stir-fry the other night.

Later, she'll wonder about the strange glow that brought her attention to that knife.

Later, she'll realize it didn't really have a source.

Not an electrical one, anyway.

Later, she'll understand that it was a different kind of energy glowing in the kitchen and illuminating the knife.

Now, without stopping to consider the source, she finds herself reaching out and grasping the handle.

Even as she holds the knife, she wonders why she picked it up. Just some crazy impulse. Because she's spooked herself into thinking she's in danger.

If you're that scared, she tells herself, you should just leave. Get out of the house, go next door, and wait for Gammy.

But another meow on the other side of the door reminds her that poor Gert is trapped in there—maybe by accident.

I have to get her out, Calla thinks. *Then I'll go next door.*

She reaches out and turns the knob.

The door creaks as it slowly opens.

"Gert?"

Calla takes a step into the room.

"Come on, kitty, where are—aaaah!"

She cries out as a human figure looms in front of her.

She feels her hand clenching the blade handle, feels it jerking into the air, arcing the blade.

Later, she'll realize that her arm seemed to move of its own accord. That if she had stopped to think about inflicting harm on another human being, she might not have been able to react.

The blade makes contact with a sickening thud.

A voice lets out an unearthly screech.

She recognizes it: a man's blood-curdling scream. Only once before in her life has she heard that terrible sound.

It came out of her father when he found out Mom was dead.

Murdered, shouts a voice somewhere in Calla's head. *She was murdered.*

The man, whoever he is, staggers through the doorway into the kitchen and collapses to the floor with a moan.

Even in the dim light spilling in from the dining room, Calla can see the purplish black bruise rimming his closed eye—a raccoon eye?—and realizes that he, too, is holding a weapon.

A cleaver whose deadly blade had undoubtedly been intended for her.

EIGHTEEN

Sunday, September 16
10:43 p.m.

His name, she learns later—much, much later, the next day—is Phil Chase. He's from Ohio, in his mid-twenties, a store clerk described by his neighbors as a quiet loner.

"Isn't that always the way?" Odelia muttered when they heard that phrase. "A quiet loner. Those are the neighbors to watch out for."

Calla couldn't help but think there weren't many neighbors of that kind in Lily Dale. Here, people are involved in each others' lives. They notice each other, care about each other, help each other . . . along with hundreds of people who show up here during the season.

Phil Chase was the one who had abducted and murdered Kaitlyn Riggs and tried to murder Erin Shannahan. When they searched his apartment, they found out that he'd also been stalking a girl named Hayley Gorzynski.

Who is currently rehearsing the role of Sandy in an Akron production of *Grease*.

That information blew Calla away.

Now she gets it. Now she has the answer to at least one question about what's been happening to her. But there are still so many others . . . along with some new ones.

Phil would have undoubtedly killed Hayley and other young girls, Calla among them, if she hadn't stopped him.

No, she didn't kill him.

She was certain he was dead when she went barreling next door to Ramona's, pounding frantically on her door and screaming for help.

Everything after that point was a blur: Ramona calling the police, the squad cars arriving with sirens wailing, the officers who asked Calla, again and again, what, exactly, had happened.

Finally, what seemed like hours later, they stopped asking questions and started answering hers.

That was when she found out she had inflicted enough injury on her would-be attacker to have left him incapacitated and unconscious . . . but alive.

Just like Erin was when they found her.

The police are sure she'll be able to identify Phil Chase, who matches her description of her attacker. When she does, he'll be going to jail for a long, long time. Maybe for the rest of his life. He isn't going to hurt anyone ever again.

"But why did he do it, Gammy?" Calla asks now as she sits in the living room with her grandmother, trying to make sense of all that happened. Gert, purring contentedly, is snuggled on her lap as Calla strokes her soft fur.

"Who knows why he did it?" Odelia shakes her head. "Evil reigns in some souls. We can't explain it. We can only beware. That's why you have to be so careful, Calla. You need to learn how to protect yourself so that—"

"I protected myself pretty well," she can't help but cut in. "Right?"

The corners of Odelia's mouth quirk a little, but she keeps her expression stern. "If you don't think I'm completely alarmed at the thought of you fighting off an armed attacker who had a hundred pounds and at least six inches on you, you're dead wrong."

"At least I'm not dead *dead*. Because I protected myself."

Odelia sighs. "You did. But you need to learn that there are other ways to protect yourself. Not just physically."

"Meaning?"

"Meaning it's time you learned what you're dealing with, Calla. Look, I know you went to Patsy's class yesterday. And I'm glad."

For a moment, as Calla figures out what to say to that, the only sound in the room is the rumble of Gert's purring and the ticking of the stately grandfather clock on the far side of the room.

Then the telephone rings. All three of them—Calla, Odelia, and even Gert—jump at the piercing interruption.

Pressing one hand against her heart as if to calm its racing, Odelia stands and reaches for the receiver with the other. "Hello? Oh, Jeff! Hi!"

Uh-oh. Here we go.

At last, Calla faces the imminent answer to the question that's been on her mind all day: How long will it take Dad, after her grandmother tells him what happened last night, to get on a plane? Or maybe just buy her a one-way ticket out of here?

She's willing to bet one of them will be packing his or her bags momentarily.

"Oh, we've been fine," Odelia says casually. "It's been a little chilly since you left, and yesterday it poured all day."

Wait a minute. Did Odelia just tell Dad they've been *fine*? And now she's talking about the weather?

Shocked, Calla catches her grandmother's eye. Odelia merely smiles at her and keeps chatting.

"Yes, she actually had a date last night with a nice boy. I've known his family for years. Hmm? Oh, he took her to a jazz concert in Buffalo. I know. Yes, she soaks up culture like a sponge, and there's plenty of it around here. I was thinking of taking her to the Albright-Knox Art Gallery in Buffalo next weekend, actually."

This is the first Calla's heard of that, and if she weren't so edgy, she'd have to smile. Odelia is laying it on thick.

Yeah, and now she's outright lying: "No, she's not here right now. She and Evangeline are out shopping with Ramona . . . Yes, from next door. Okay, I'll tell them you said hello. Of course I'll give Calla your love. Sure, I'll have her call you back tomorrow since it might be too late when she gets back tonight. What? Oh, right, the time change. Well, sure, I'll try to remember to tell her. You know how forgetful I can be, though, so don't worry if you don't hear from her until tomorrow . . . Okay, 'bye, Jeff."

She hangs up, looking pleased with herself.

"Why did you do that, Gammy?"

"Because it was necessary. I thought you might be too exhausted to take a phone call right now."

"When are we going to tell him what happened?"

"Who's going to tell him? Not me."

"So, you want me to do it, then?" Calla asks slowly, trying to wrap her mind around the situation. "Is that it?"

Odelia tilts her head. "Do you *want* to tell him?"

"Are you kidding me?" Calla frowns. Does she dare believe her grandmother is going to keep this a secret? That's too good to be true.

"Look, if we tell him," Odelia says matter-of-factly, "he'll pull you out of here so fast your head will spin. He won't understand that with that horrible man in jail, you're as safe here as you are anywhere."

Calla exhales shakily. Odelia is right. The danger—that particular danger, anyway—is past.

Dad definitely won't see it that way if he finds out, though.

Which he won't, if she and her grandmother don't tell him. After Phil Chase was able to track her down thanks to the *Dispatch* article, the authorities promised to keep the press out of it this time. Calla was assured that her name, and any identifying details about her, won't appear in the papers.

"The thing is," her grandmother goes on, "it would be much more dangerous for you to be removed from Lily Dale and thrown into a world where you'll have no spiritual guidance whatsoever. Here, I can keep an eye on you and you can begin with Patsy's class and learn how to use your psychic abilities responsibly."

"So, you want me to stay, then?"

"Of course. But more than that . . . you *need* to stay."

"I thought you were going to be angry with me because . . . well, because I didn't tell you about those visions I was having. With Kaitlyn. And that I called the tip line about Erin."

"And saved a life." Odelia sighs heavily. "Listen, I know what it's like to see things you don't understand . . . and to hide those things from everyone else because you don't know what they mean, or you're scared out of your mind, or you're embarrassed and you think you're some kind of freak. I need to set you on the right path. When I think about what might have happened to you . . ."

"But it didn't happen."

"But it could have," Odelia says firmly, and holds her close. "And it's partly my fault. I kept feeling it—that you were in some kind of danger—and what did I do?"

"It doesn't matter. I'm okay."

"It does matter. You almost weren't okay. But you're going to be safe here from now on, Calla. Lily Dale is the place for you right now and I'm going to do everything I can to see that you stay for as long as you need to. Now go get some sleep."

In her mother's old bedroom, Calla quickly changes into her pajamas, realizing she hasn't slept in almost two full days.

Catching sight of her reflection in the mirror above the dresser, she notices that her face looks gaunt and drawn, with deep circles under her bloodshot eyes.

Oh, geez. You've definitely looked better, she tells herself, quickly turning away.

Her gaze falls on the jewelry box. She hesitates for a moment, then opens the lid for the first time in days.

The remnants of that haunting tune spill out in hesitant, tinkling notes as the brass key on the bottom winds down.

She doesn't bother to rewind it. She doesn't care if she ever hears that melody again.

The emerald bracelet is still tucked inside the box.

Well, of course it is. Where else would it be? This is where you left it, remember?

Yeah.

She also remembers that the bracelet seems to have a life of its own, popping up out of nowhere in the night. Who's to say it won't disappear again?

Frowning at the thought, Calla snatches it and wraps it securely around her left wrist, snapping the clasp. She tugs it gently a few times, and it holds. Good.

Maybe you should start wearing it again after all, she tells herself. *Maybe it'll help you feel closer to her.*

She runs her fingers over the glossy green stones and can't help but notice that they seem to feel oddly warm. Almost as if . . .

Okay, now you're delirious.

It's been such a long, difficult day.

But it's over now, she tells herself, yawning deeply as she folds back the quilt made of fabric squares from her mother's childhood dresses.

A sense of calm begins to seep into her aching body as she slips into bed.

You can relax now.

Yes. At last she can escape, if only for a little while, the lingering memory of what happened to her last night.

She runs her fingertips over her mother's emerald bracelet, trying to clear her brain.

All she needs to do now is go . . . to . . . sleep . . .

But she can't.

A telltale chill is creeping into the room like an unwelcome night visitor.

Oh, no, Calla thinks wearily, reluctant to open her eyes. *Please, no. Not tonight. I'm so exhausted.*

She burrows deeper into the covers, hoping that if she ignores it—whoever, *whatever* it is—it will go away.

But she can feel persistent goose bumps raising the hair on her arms, and the air is quickly becoming saturated with a presence determined to make itself known.

Finally, Calla allows her eyes to open.

A figure is clearly visible in the darkened room, a few feet from the bed, watching her.

Calla recognizes the apparition in a flash: Kaitlyn Riggs.

But this time, for the first time ever, she's smiling. Their eyes meet and she gives a little nod at Calla.

Thank you.

Kaitlyn's heartfelt words echo in Calla's head as she begins to fade.

"You're welcome," Calla whispers, and she adds one last "Good-bye" before Kaitlyn disappears entirely.

Knowing she'll never see her again, Calla feels a twinge of sadness, yet mostly just relief.

She yawns and allows her body to relax once again, her

right hand wrapped comfortingly around the bracelet on her opposite wrist. The stones really do feel warm.

It's just the heat of your skin, she tells herself drowsily as she drifts off. *That's all . . .*

Her mother is waiting for her in a dream.

Stephanie is in the professionally decorated, tropical-hued master bedroom in their house back in Tampa, getting dressed for work.

Watching her, a conscious part of Calla's brain is aware, somehow, that her mother thinks she's alone in the house . . . yet she isn't.

A helpless voyeur, she watches her mother slip into a familiar pencil-slim charcoal gray skirt, then the matching suit jacket. Mom hums to herself as she fastens the row of round, shiny black buttons, then steps into a pair of high-heeled black Gucci pumps.

Turning to her bureau, she reaches for the bottle of Calvin Klein perfume she always wore—she called it her signature scent. Calla sees the label on the bottle: it's called Eternity.

Mom sprays it, and Calla's nostrils fill with the unmistakable smell of lilies of the valley.

But how can that be? It doesn't make sense, Calla thinks fuzzily. Eternity smells spicy, almost fruity. Nothing like lilies of the valley.

That's because you're dreaming. Dreams don't always make sense.

Then again . . .

This doesn't feel like a dream.

At first, it was almost as though she were watching a scene in a movie. But now, wrapped in the familiar floral scent that couldn't have come out of a Calvin Klein bottle, Calla is gradually understanding that it's all too real.

She can vividly see every detail in the bedroom; can hear the far-off sound of the sprinkler system hissing across the lawn two stories beneath the closed window; can feel her feet walking in those tight, tall shoes.

Yes, suddenly, she, Calla, is actually in the scene. Living it. She has morphed into her mother, has gone from bystander to experiencing the action through her mother's eyes.

She reaches toward the king-sized bed and lifts the edge of the Caribbean-blue quilt. Her fingers probe deep into the crevice between mattress and box spring. At last she finds it and pulls it out.

A manila envelope.

For a moment, she just looks at it, shaking her head.

Then she whispers aloud into the empty room, "I'm sorry. I have to do this."

Leaving the room with the envelope in hand, she moves down the hall past the slightly open door to Calla's room, toward the stairs.

Only when she's passed the bedroom and reached the head of the stairs does it occur to her that Calla's door should be closed. Puzzled, she starts to turn to look back.

In that stark, sickening, awful flash, she realizes that the door is now fully open, that someone was lurking there, that whoever it is has come up behind her and—

Before she can see who it is, a pair of hands land roughly on her shoulders and push, hard.

She lets out a shrill, terrifying scream.

Then she's falling, hurtling through space at first, then

beginning to hit the hard wooden steps, and bounce, and hit again, screaming as bones shatter and flesh is bruised and torn open and ferocious pain explodes within—

With a gasp, Calla sits up in bed, her heart pounding frantically.

Oh. Oh, thank God.

Dazed, she realizes that she's safe.

In Lily Dale.

In Mom's girlhood bed, beneath a quilt made from dresses Mom once wore, her mother's emerald bracelet on her arm.

She shudders, recalling every detail of a horrific nightmare that may not have been a nightmare at all.

Because it felt real.

So real it was almost like . . .

A memory?

Not her own, though.

Mom's.

Did Calla just relive her mother's last moments on earth?

If so, then it really was murder.

The envelope—it had to be the one Darrin gave her. What was in it?

She was holding it when she fell. Calla was the one who found her at the foot of the stairs that awful day. There was no envelope. She'd have seen it. There was nothing but her mother's broken, bloodied corpse.

Someone wanted Stephanie Lauder Delaney dead. Someone pushed her to her death, then disappeared with the envelope.

Who?

And why?

Calla takes a deep breath, exhales shakily, her entire body trembling as she realizes what she has to do.

It's time to use Lisa's airline voucher and book a flight back to Tampa to do some digging around.

I'll find out what really happened. I promise you that, Mom. I'll find out who did this to you . . . and I'll make sure someone pays. Just like Phil Chase.

AUTHOR'S NOTE

Growing up near Lily Dale, I was always fascinated by the mediums whose life work involved breaching the veil between the living and the dead. I perceived them as an enigmatic, magical group—closed off, of course, to us mere mortals.

When, as an author, I began my professional research into the birthplace of spiritualism—and the spiritualists in Lily Dale—I was in for a surprise. The mediums couldn't have been more welcoming or more willing to share their insights into the many connections between their world, my world, and, of course, the Other Side. They don't subscribe to the magical mystic vs. mere mortal theory. According to them, while some of us are inherently more perceptive to spirit energy, we all have the ability to open ourselves to it. Just as with any other skill, it requires education, dedication, and practice.

Like Calla in *Believing*, I was invited last March to sit in on an off-season Beginning Mediumship class in Lily Dale. My husband, Mark, insisted on driving me the ten remote, hilly miles from my hometown. I'll confess that while I protested being chaperoned, I was secretly grateful. Lily Dale in broad daylight at the height of the summer season can be a spooky place. Imagine it off-season, on an icy, stormy night—which of course it was.

Planning to wait in the car parked in the lakeside lot, Mark first walked me through the dark streets lined with largely deserted Victorian cottages to the class at the octagonal Mediums League building. There, we found an eclectic group gathered in a circle around a flickering candle.

Let me point out that my husband is a quiet, unassuming, tremendously supportive guy who regards my novelist research adventures with amusement—preferably from the sidelines. But the fledgling mediums wouldn't hear of Mark waiting in the car for two hours. Nor—when he attempted to sit in a corner—would they hear of him breaking the circle. Flashing me a The Things I Do for You glare, Mark took his place in the circle.

As the class progressed, led by Registered Medium Donna Riegel, we found ourselves completely engaged. When it came time for a hands-on exercise in billet-reading, we assumed we were just bystanders, but Donna invited us to give it a whirl. I was eager to try; my husband was—predictably— embarrassed and reluctant.

Everyone privately wrote something on a slip of paper and put it into a bowl. In darkness, we passed it around and everyone took one. Clasping the folded slips, we meditated under Donna's direction, asking the spirits to show us the answers to whatever was written there. Then, one by one, we tried to channel unseen energy to "read" the papers, or billets, without looking at them.

Mark's turn came quickly. He said nervously, "I obviously don't know what I'm doing, so . . ." Donna encouraged him to try anyway. He confessed, "All I saw in my head was the name Jenn—spelled with two *n*'s. J-E-N-N. That's it." Donna told him to open the paper. Prominently written on it was the name Jeanne. J-E-A-N-N-E. We were all—including Mark—fairly astounded at how close he had come.

I still tease my husband about having missed his psychic calling, and about putting up a shingle and taking up residence in Lily Dale. But the truth is, faced with the spiritualist philosophy that we are all capable of channeling unseen energy, I have to say . . . I, like Calla, find myself believing.

NATIONAL BESTSELLING AUTHOR

WENDY
CORSI
STAUB

LILY DALE
CONNECTING

The apparition has popped up a few times here in Lily Dale since Calla first spotted her at Mom's funeral in Tampa last summer.

As always, she's dressed in flowing white, with black hair pulled back from her exotic face and dark eyes that aren't unkind. Just . . . intense. Wafting in the air is the distinct floral scent that usually accompanies her—lilies of the valley.

Jacy Bly, who lives across Melrose Park from Odelia's house and knows all about these things, said she's probably Calla's spirit guide. He, like the locals, believes that everyone has guides, which as far as Calla can tell, are spiritualism's version of guardian angels.

"Calla?" Lisa is asking in her ear. "Hello-o?"

Aiyana.

The unfamiliar Native American word, which Jacy later told her means "forever flowering," popped into Calla's head out of nowhere one day. It's the spirit guide's name. Calla's not sure how she knows that; she just does. She's as positive about it as she is that Aiyana has been trying to tell her something.

Something about Mom's death.

That, Calla figured out—with Jacy's help—is why Aiyana's presence brings the scent of lilies of the valley, Stephanie's favorite flower.

If only she'd bring Mom with her.

A sorrowful tide of longing sweeps through Calla as she imagines what it would be like to come face-to-face with her mother again right here, right now . . .

Or anywhere, ever again.

She hears another distant boom of thunder and from the corner of her eye, sees a flicker of movement across the room.

Calla turns her head just in time to see a book fly off the stack on the coffee table and land on the floor, pages fluttering open as it lands.

Taken aback, she looks at Aiyana. "Did you do that?"

Aiyana just gazes at her, beginning to look a lot less solid than she did a few moments ago.

Calla read somewhere that it takes a lot of energy for a spirit to move an object around a room. Why would Aiyana even bother with a stupid parlor trick now?

Calla is long past needing proof of otherworldly powers. She gets it. Aiyana's from the Other Side. She doesn't need to throw books on the floor to prove herself.

"Wait . . . before you go . . . I just need to know what happened to her," she tells Aiyana fervently, realizing she's fading fast. "You have to help me. Please."

"Oh, Calla . . ." That's Lisa, on the other end of the phone line, suddenly sounding somber and emotional. "I will—I'll help you. Whatever you need. I'm here for you, I promise."

Calla wasn't talking to Lisa.

But all at once, Aiyana is gone, and Lisa is offering to help, and God knows she needs it.

"Remember how I told you I'd come to Florida to visit?"

"Yeah . . . please don't tell me your father changed his mind about letting you come." Calla's father, Jeff, is a physics professor on sabbatical at Shellborne College in California, and Lisa knows how overprotective he can be. Especially lately.

"No, it's just . . . if you really will help me do this . . . I need you."

"To do what?"

"When I get there, we can go over to my house and see if we can find any evidence that someone was out to get my mother."

"Evidence?" Lisa laughs nervously. "Who are we, CSI?"

"This isn't a joke, Lis'!"

"I know, I know, I'm sorry. I know it isn't. And I want you to come down so I can help you. Just . . . um, well, what about school?"

She's freaked out, Calla realizes. She doesn't want to get involved.

And I can't blame her, really.

"Listen," Calla says, "you don't have to do this with me. I know it's—"

"No, I want to help you," Lisa cuts in firmly. "Whatever you need. So, when are you coming?"

Calla smiles. Good old Lisa won't let her down. "I don't know . . . it'll have to be on a weekend. Maybe Friday?"

"This coming Friday? That would be—oh, wait, my parents said we might go up to Tallahassee to visit the campus again."

Florida State, Calla knows, is Lisa's self-proclaimed "safety" school—though her brother, Kevin, once privately told Calla that with Lisa's grades, even Florida State might be a "reach" school.

"But—ooh, I know! You can come with us and maybe we can both check out the sororities and—"

"No, I really just need to be in Tampa, to see what I can find out," Calla says impatiently. Lisa apparently doesn't grasp that this is a return to the scene of a crime and not a carefree vacation.

"What are you going to do there, exactly?"

"Well, my father said I can get my mother's laptop to use here, remember? I'm thinking there might be something in her files if I can get into them. She used her laptop for everything—work, paying bills, shopping, making travel arrangements. I feel like I might find out more about what was going on with her toward the end. My father told me she wasn't herself the last few months—she was really detached from him, but he wasn't sure why."

"Yeah, and the other thing is, once you have the laptop, we'll be able to stay in touch better, and you can get back onto MySpace," Lisa says excitedly, and Calla fights back a sigh.

Lisa truly doesn't realize that there's something far more significant at stake here than the Internet access that was so hard to live without when Calla first came to Lily Dale.

More evidence that Calla really is part of a world far different than Lisa's—and the one she herself left behind not so very long ago. But it seems like a lifetime has passed since Calla was living in the big, upscale Tampa home with both her parents, going to private school, dating Kevin Wilson . . .

"Well, how about if you come down next weekend?" Lisa suggests.

"Yeah, I guess I—" She breaks off, remembering.

"What?"

"That's the homecoming dance, and someone asked me to go." Funny how something that seemed so important just days ago now seems trivial.

Not to Lisa, though. She squeals in Calla's ear. "Who was it? Blue or Jacy?"

Lisa, of course, knows all about the two local guys who are, sort of, involved in Calla's love life at the moment. What she doesn't know is that Calla still hasn't quite gotten over Lisa's brother, Kevin, now a sophomore at Cornell. He dumped her back in April, after he found a new girlfriend in college. Last week, though, he popped up in Calla's e-mail, sounding like he wants to be friends. Or maybe more.

"Blue asked me to homecoming," she tells Lisa, firmly shoving Kevin from her thoughts.

"Blue—is he the hot one?"

"Actually, they both are." She smiles wistfully, thinking about quiet, enigmatic Jacy, who almost kissed her once.

But Blue Slayton is the one who *did* kiss her, and who asked her to the dance. And that's what counts, right?

Right. And it's really not that trivial. Calla has to have a normal life, right? Despite living in this crazy town surrounded by ghosts and people who can talk to them. Despite needing to know what really happened to Mom.

"So is Blue, like, the star quarterback on the football team for the homecoming game?" Lisa wants to know.

"I hate to burst your bubble, but no. He doesn't play football. He's one of the best players on the soccer team, though."

And Jacy runs cross-country.

She doesn't say that part out loud. They're not talking about Jacy; they're talking about Blue.

Funny, she's actually been considering going to one of Jacy's meets, but she hasn't had a chance—or, okay, much motivation—to get herself to one of Blue's soccer games.

They're playing away this weekend, but there's a home match the night before homecoming. She definitely needs to go.

Lisa asks a few more questions about Blue and the dance and what Calla's going to wear.

"Who knows? I'm clueless. It's not like I have a closet full of stuff to choose from, or a mall around the corner, or any cash if there were one."

"Well, maybe your grandmother will take you shopping for a dress. Just don't let her pick it out." Having visited Lily Dale, Lisa's met Odelia, with her red hair, cat's-eye glasses, and preference for loud, mismatched wardrobe colors.

"Ramona said she'd take me to the mall in Buffalo," Calla muses aloud, watching Gert curl up into a purring ball once again. The cat keeps one green eye open and focused on the spot where Aiyana appeared—and disappeared.

"Ramona?"

"Taggart. My next-door neighbor. My friend Evangeline's

aunt, who's raising her and her brother—I think I told you about them, right?"

"Mmm . . . maybe." Sounds like Lisa is losing interest. Or maybe she's jealous.

"Ramona's great, and she said she'd take me shopping, and she's going to treat me to a haircut, too, if I want. God knows I really need one." Calla shoves her thick, overgrown bangs back from her forehead and glances in the antique mirror above the chintz sofa.

Her long brown hair typically doesn't require much care, but she's definitely getting split ends from three months of neglect, and her streaks of gold highlights are fading fast here in generally overcast western New York State.

It's not just her hair that needs help after a month in Lily Dale. There are deep shadows beneath her wide-set hazel eyes, thanks to a string of restless nights. Her face is pale; the faint freckles that used to dust her nose are gone, thank goodness, but so is the healthy glow cast by the Florida sun.

If she's going to go to the homecoming dance with one of the most popular guys in the senior class, she'd better do something about the way she looks.

"So this woman you barely know is taking you shopping and for a haircut? That's really nice of her, especially now that you don't have . . ." Lisa trails off.

Your mom, she was going to say.

That hard lump is back in Calla's throat, aching so that she can't find the words to respond, even if just to tell Lisa that Ramona Taggart isn't someone she "barely knows."

For one thing, friendships form fast here in Lily Dale. For

another, Ramona knew Calla's mother well, having grown up right next door, just a few years younger than Stephanie. Calla has felt a connection to her from the moment they met—and to her orphaned niece, Evangeline.

Lisa changes the subject, sort of. "So, when can you come down here? Let's make a plan so I'll have something to look forward to."

Again, Calla bristles, wanting to tell Lisa that this is no vacation.

Instead, she says only, "I guess maybe I can come the weekend after homecoming, even though that seems way too far away. I'll check with my grandmother and my dad and let you know, okay?"

"Okay. But meanwhile, Calla . . . I feel like that place is really getting to you. Like you're dwelling on too much of this dark stuff all of a sudden. Maybe you should just, you know . . . leave."

Calla, who mere weeks ago wanted more than anything to get the heck out of Lily Dale, shoots back, "Leave? No way!"

Just the other night, she and her grandmother had that long conversation about why she needs to stay, and how Odelia is going to guide her, teach her how to handle this unwanted, obviously hereditary, so-called gift of hers.

She can't tell Lisa about the terrifying events that led up to the conversation, though. She and her grandmother agreed never to discuss with anyone what happened last Saturday night. Especially Dad, who would yank her out of Lily Dale immediately if he knew. The police promised to keep it out of the newspapers, for safety's sake.

So no one—other than Ramona, upon whose door Calla banged, hysterical, in the wee hours—had to know about the serial killer who decided to make Calla his next victim after she—with a little help from one of his victims on the Other Side—led the police to a teenage girl he'd left for dead.

Even now, over a week later, she shudders when she thinks about what could have happened to her at his hands.

But it didn't happen. I'm all right.

"I don't know how you can stand to live in a place like that," Lisa drawls on, "but if you're staying, I just hope you can manage to get past all this dark stuff."

"I will."

"Call me when you decide what day you're coming, okay?"

"Okay," Calla promises. "I'll see you."

"Yeah. And, hey, don't forget I love you."

"I love you, too," Calla returns, as always, before they hang up.

Hugging herself as if that can possibly banish the hollow feeling inside, she goes back over to the window.

The sky is blackening quickly beyond the leafy branches and gabled rooftops of Cottage Row. Calla turns her head, hoping to spot her grandmother attempting to beat the rain, hurrying home through Melrose Park from her afternoon mediums' league meeting.

No sign of Odelia, though; the street and park are deserted, as are quite a few of the shuttered, clearly abandoned pastel Victorian cottages across the green.

Just a few weeks ago, with the official summer season still under way, the town was teeming with activity.

Every July and August, people come from all over the world to visit the local mediums in search of their dearly departed or psychic counseling or spiritual healing. Then September rolls around, and not only does the steady stream of visitors cease—literally overnight—but a good many of the locals disappear as well.

Not Calla's grandmother. With maybe a hundred others, ODELIA LAUDER, REGISTERED MEDIUM—as the hand-painted shingle above her front porch refers to her—is a year-round resident of the gated little lakeside town whose claim to fame is being the birthplace of spiritualism and that remains almost entirely populated by psychic mediums.

Spotting movement across the green, Calla realizes it's not deserted after all.

A man has materialized, walking slowly along the street, leaning on a cane. For a few moments, Calla isn't sure whether he's alive or dead—his wind-whipped overcoat and brimmed hat could be from another era.

But having grown up in Florida, land of retirees, Calla realizes he might just like to dress in old-fashioned, formal clothes. A lot of elderly gents do.

She watches him stop at a house across the street, look at the sign that reads REV. DORIS HENDERSON, CLAIRVOYANT.

He hesitates only a moment before painstakingly making his way up the steps to the door.

Watching him, Calla doesn't have to be psychic to know Doris won't be home. She's at the mediums' league meeting with Odelia and just about everyone else in town.

Sure enough, after several knocks and a lengthy wait at

Doris's door, the man gingerly descends the stairs and shuffles on down the street.

He's looking for a reading, Calla realizes, as he stops at the next house that bears a shingle advertising a spiritualist in residence. No answer there, either.

Odelia's house is next on his path, and sure enough, he's heading deliberately—and with obvious effort—for her door, poor guy.

When Calla opens it, he's visibly relieved that the exertion wasn't in vain.

Tipping his hat to reveal a robust head of salt-and-pepper hair, he says, "Good afternoon, Ms. Lauder."

"Oh, I'm not her . . . I'm her granddaughter."

"Owen Henry." He extends a surprisingly firm handshake for such a feeble-looking guy. "Pleased to meet you."

"Calla," she supplies.

"Calla. Like the lily. And you're just as lovely."

Standing here in her jeans and hoodie, she doesn't feel as lovely as a lily, but he's a charming old guy and she can't help but smile and thank him.

"Is your grandmother home? I'm afraid I'm in need of her services to reach someone very dear to me."

Ordinarily—especially after what happened to her Saturday night—Calla wouldn't freely admit to being alone in the house, but this guy is obviously harmless. And in emotional pain, judging by the sad expression in his eyes.

"She's not here right now. Sorry. But if you want to leave me your phone number, I can have her get in touch with you and set up an appointment."

He brightens and offers a heartfelt, "Thank you. I'm desperate to get in touch with my wife, my sweet Betty."

As he says the name, a vision flashes into Calla's head. Just a quick glimpse of an elderly woman with a puff of white hair and gold-rimmed eyeglasses on a chain.

Betty?

She doesn't dare mention it. Not after what happened the last time she got involved with one of Odelia's clients, Elaine Riggs.

After taking down the man's name and phone number, she sends him on his way.

Then it's back to moping around until her grandmother comes home at last, about a half hour later. Thank goodness. It's hard to stay glum with Odelia around.

Today, she has on a bright pink-and-white polka-dotted raincoat that clashes with her dyed red hair and purple cat's-eye glasses, along with green rubber rain boots covered in yellow polka dots.

Calla, who was once mortified by her grandmother's wardrobe style, now knows exactly how Odelia's mind was working when she pulled together the outfit. The theme is polka dots—who cares about clashing colors? Not Odelia, who's also wearing red lipstick and toting a teal canvas bag. And—surprise, surprise—she's carrying on an animated conversation with . . . nobody.

At least, nobody Calla can see.

In any other town, the casual onlooker might decide her grandmother is in obvious need of a psychiatrist.

Here in Lily Dale, no one bats an eye at conversations with invisible partners.

Watching her grandmother throw back her head and laugh heartily at whatever it is the spirit is telling her, Calla can't help but grin.

Thank God for Odelia.

"Happy Monday," she calls cheerfully from the hall a minute later, shutting the door behind her. "I beat the rain, but just barely. What's new?"

"Someone came by for a reading. I told him you'd get back to him. He was a widower, and he's really desperate to reach his wife."

"Aren't they all," Odelia murmurs, shaking her head as she pockets Owen Henry's contact information. "How was school?"

"Fine," Calla says automatically.

Hmm, come to think of it, how was school?

Let's see, she got an A on her social studies test, an A– on her art project, and a D on her math quiz.

Okay . . . not so fine.

Odelia appears in the doorway. Her coat is gone, and Calla isn't surprised to see that she's wearing a navy-and-white polka-dotted blouse with her jeans, which are cuffed at the knees—the better to show off the rubber boots, naturally.

"I just saw Patsy Metcalf at the meeting," she tells Calla, "and she asked me if you'll be at her beginning mediumship class again tomorrow morning."

"What did you say?"

"What do you think? I said absolutely. I told her to enroll you for the rest of the course."

"Gammy, I don't know if I want—"

"Remember what we talked about the other night? I told

you I'm going to help you learn how to use your psychic abilities responsibly, and you're going to start with Patsy's class," Odelia says firmly, and steps around the book on the floor on her way to pet Gert.

Funny, Calla's mother would have stooped to pick it up. Most people would, actually.

Not Odelia. She's not the most meticulous housekeeper in the world, and her house is jam-packed with more stuff than any human being could ever use in one lifetime—not that Odelia believes in anyone having just one lifetime.

As her grandmother scoops the kitten into her arms, Calla leans over to pick up the book, then stops short.

It's one she checked out of the local library a few days ago, a thick, musty-smelling volume on the history of Lily Dale.

"What the heck is this doing down here?" she wonders aloud.

Odelia glances at it. "What is that?"

"My library book. I had it upstairs, on my bookshelf. Did you borrow it?"

"No."

"Then how did it get down here?"

"Miriam? Did you do that?" Odelia calls good-naturedly. No reply.

"What did she say?" Calla asks.

"She didn't say anything."

"Well, actually, she was just here a few minutes ago."

Odelia raises a dyed red eyebrow. "You saw her?"

"Sort of. I caught a glimpse of someone flitting by out of the corner of my eye, over there." She gestures at the doorway.

Odelia nods approvingly. "That's how it is, in the beginning. Sooner or later, you'll begin to see them more clearly."

Calla wants to remind her that she already *has* seen—and spoken to—apparitions.

But then she might be tempted to mention Aiyana, and she still isn't ready to share that with her grandmother. Not until she knows more about what might have happened to her mother.

Part of her reasoning is that Odelia, who has already warned her not to get involved in criminal cases, would be livid if she thought Calla was disobeying her orders, especially after what happened the other night.

The other thing is . . .

Well, Mom and Odelia didn't get along, and she isn't sure why. Out of a sense of loyalty to her mother, Calla needs to keep some things private for now.

"I'm going to go see if we have anything I can whip up for dinner," Odelia says, and heads for the kitchen with Gert in her arms.

As she picks up the book, Calla glances at the yellowed pages.

When it fell, it opened to a map of Lily Dale.

A mark jumps out at her—a circled X, made in old-fashioned sepia-toned ink.

She recognizes that it would be located in a wooded area near the pet cemetery and a woodland trail that leads through the Leolyn Woods to Inspiration Stump.

The first time Calla heard that an old tree stump, now encased in concrete, marks Lily Dale's most hallowed ground, she rolled her eyes. Leave it to the New Age freaks to pay homage to a nondescript hunk of cement.

Was that blatant disdain really only a few weeks ago?

Now she's been to the stump, buried deep in a grove of ancient trees, fronted by rows of benches as though it's a solitary performer on some eerie primordial stage. During the season, it's where the audience, hopeful of making contact with lost loved ones, gathers to be read by the mediums.

Maybe the constant collective wave of grief and longing contributes to the highly charged atmosphere there.

Or maybe it's something more mystical, more otherworldly than that.

"Do you want me to find that spot?" Calla whispers to Aiyana, wherever she is. "The place marked on the map? Is that why you dropped the book?"

The only answer is a flash of lightning, followed by a deafening boom of thunder and the rattle of rain on the roof as the storm moves in.

Leolyn Woods?

It'll have to wait.

WENDY CORSI STAUB grew up in New York, just a few miles from the real town of Lily Dale. As a teenager, she and her friends visited the mediums there, hoping to find out whom they would marry. One medium told Wendy that her future husband's name would begin with the letters M-A. She wrote down the medium's prediction and forgot about it until years later, when she found her notes from that reading. By then she was married to her husband, Mark.

Wendy has published more than sixty books for adults and teenagers and is a *New York Times* bestselling author of several suspense novels. She lives in Westchester, New York, with her husband and their two sons.

Visit her Web sites at
www.wendycorsistaub.com
www.myspace.com/lilydalebooks
www.myspace.com/wendytheauthor